The
Best
Mistake

The
Best
Mistake

Nora Roberts

THORNDIKE
CHIVERS

This Large Print edition is published by Thorndike Press®, Waterville, Maine USA and by BBC Audiobooks Ltd, Bath, England.

Published in 2005 in the U.S. by arrangement with Harlequin Books S.A.

Published in 2005 in the U.K. by arrangement with Harlequin Enterprises II B.V.

U.S.   Hardcover   0-7862-7991-5   (Americana)
U.K.   Hardcover   1-4056-3553-3   (Chivers Large Print)
U.K.   Softcover   1-4056-3554-1   (Camden Large Print)

The text of this Large Print edition is unabridged.
Other aspects of the book may vary from the original edition.

Set in 18 pt. Plantin by Al Chase.

Printed in the United States on permanent paper.

British Library Cataloguing-in-Publication Data available

Library of Congress Cataloging-in-Publication Data

Roberts, Nora.
  The best mistake / by Nora Roberts.
    p. cm. — (Thorndike Press large print Americana)
  ISBN 0-7862-7991-5 (lg. print : hc : alk. paper)
  1. Single mothers — Fiction.   2. Large type books.   I. Title.
  II. Thorndike Press large print Americana series.
PS3568.O243B47 2005
813'.54—dc22   2005016542

The
Best
Mistake

Chapter 1

No one answered the door. Coop glanced at the scrawled note in his hand to make sure he had the right address. It checked out, and since the tidy two-story Tudor in the neat, tree-lined neighborhood was precisely what he was after, he knocked again. Loudly.

There was a car in the drive, an aging station wagon that could use a good wash and a little bodywork. Somebody was in there, he thought, scowling up at the second-floor window, where music pumped out — high-volume rock with a thumping backbeat. He stuffed the note and his hands in his pockets and took a moment to survey the surroundings.

The house was trim, set nicely off the road behind clipped bayberry hedges. The flower garden, in which spring blossoms were beginning to thrive, was both colorful and just wild enough not to look static.

Not that he was a big flower lover, but there *was* something to be said for ambience.

There was a shiny red tricycle beside the driveway, and that made him a little uneasy. He wasn't particularly fond of kids. Not that he disliked them. It was just that they always seemed a kind of foreign entity to him, like aliens from an outlying planet: they spoke a different language, had a different culture. And, well, they were short, and usually sticky.

Still, the ad had talked of quiet, privacy, and a convenient distance from Baltimore. That was exactly what he was looking for.

He knocked again, only to have a thundering wave of music wash out the window over him. The rock didn't bother him. At least he understood it. But he wasn't a man to kick his heels outside a closed door for long, so he tried the knob.

When it turned, he pushed the door open and walked in. In an old habit, he pushed back the dark hair that fell over his forehead and scanned the none-too-neat living room he'd entered.

There was a lot of clutter, and he, a bachelor who'd spent a great deal of his thirty-two years living alone, wondered over it. He wasn't fussy or obsessive, he often told himself. It was simply that everything had a place, and it was easier to find if it had been put there. Obviously his prospective landlord didn't agree.

There were toys that went along with the tricycle outside, piles of magazines and newspapers, a pint-size fielder's cap that declared for the O's.

At least the kid had taste, Coop decided, and moved on.

There was a small powder room done in an amazing combination of purple and green, and a den that had been converted into a makeshift office. File drawers were open, papers spilling out. In the kitchen dishes waited in the sink to be washed, and lurid drawings, created by a child with a wild imagination, decorated the front of the refrigerator.

Maybe, he thought, it was just as well no one had answered the door.

He considered backtracking and wandering upstairs. As long as he was here, it made sense to check the rest of the place out. Instead, he stepped outside to get the lay of the land. He spotted open wooden steps leading to a short deck. The private entrance the ad had mentioned, he mused, and climbed.

The glass door was open, and the music rolling through it was over-whelming. He caught the smell of fresh paint, one he'd always enjoyed, and stepped inside.

The open area combined kitchen and living space cleverly enough. The appliances weren't new, but they were gleaming. The tile floor had been scrubbed recently enough for him to identify pine cleaner beneath the scent of paint.

Feeling more hopeful, he followed the music, snooping a bit as he went. The bathroom was as scrupulously clean as the kitchen, and, fortunately, a plain glossy white. Beside the sink was a book on home repair, open to the plumbing section. Wary, Coop turned on the tap. When the water flowed out fast and clear, he nodded, satisfied.

A small room with definite office potential and a nice view of the yard was across the hall. The ad had claimed two bedrooms.

The music led him to it, a fair-sized room that fronted the house, with space enough for his California king. The floor, which seemed to be a random-width oak in good condition, was covered with splattered drop cloths. There were paint cans, trays, brushes, extra rollers. A laborer in baggy overalls and bare feet completed the picture. Despite the hair-concealing cap and oversize denim, Coop recognized a woman when he saw one.

She was tall, and the bare feet on the stepladder were long and narrow and decorated with paint splotches and hot-pink toenails. She sang, badly, along with the music.

Coop rapped on the door jamb. "Excuse me."

She went on painting, her hips moving rhythmically as she started on the ceiling border. Stepping across the drop cloths, Coop tapped her on the back.

She screamed, jumped and turned all at once. Though he was quick on his feet, he wasn't fast enough to avoid the slap of the paintbrush across his cheek.

He swore and jerked backward, then forward again to catch her before she tumbled off the ladder. He had a quick, and not unpleasant, impression of a slim body, a pale, triangular face dominated by huge, long-lashed brown eyes, and the scent of honeysuckle.

Then he was grunting and stumbling backward, clutching the stomach her elbow had jammed into. She yelled something while he fought to get his breath back.

"Are you crazy?" he managed, then shot up a hand as she hefted a can, slopping paint over the sides as she prepared to use it as a weapon. "Lady, if you throw that at me, I'm going to have to hurt you."

"What?" she shouted.

"I said, don't throw that. I'm here about the ad."

"What?" she shouted again. Her eyes were still wide and full of panic, and she looked capable of anything.

"The ad, damn it." Still rubbing his stomach, Coop marched to the portable stereo and shut it off. "I'm here about the ad," he repeated, his voice loud in the sudden silence.

The big brown eyes narrowed with suspicion. "What ad?"

"The apartment." He swiped a hand over his cheek, studied the smear of white on it, and swore again. "The apartment."

"Really?" She kept her eyes glued

15

to his. He looked tough, she thought. Like a brawler with those broad shoulders, lean athletic build and long legs. His eyes, a light, almost translucent green, looked anything but friendly, and the faded Baltimore Orioles T-shirt and battered jeans didn't contribute any sense of respectability. She figured she could outrun him, and she could certainly outscream him. "The ad doesn't start to run until tomorrow."

"Tomorrow?" Nonplussed, he reached into his pocket for his scribbled note. "This is the right address. The ad was for this place."

She stood her ground. "It doesn't run until tomorrow, so I don't see how you could know about it."

"I work at the paper." Moving cautiously, he held out the note. "Since

I've been looking for a place, I asked one of the girls in Classifieds to keep an eye out." He glanced down at his note again. "Two-bedroom apartment on second floor, private entrance, quiet neighborhood convenient for commuters."

She only continued to frown at him. "That's right."

Realizing his inside track wasn't strictly ethical, he winced. "Look, I guess she got a little overenthusiastic. I gave her a couple of tickets to a game, and she must've figured she'd do me a favor and pass the information along a little early."

When he saw that her grip on the can had relaxed, he tried a smile. "I knocked, then I came around back." Probably best not to mention he'd wandered through the house first.

"The ad didn't run the address."

"I work at the paper," he repeated. He was taking a good look at her now. There was something vaguely familiar about her face. And what a face it was. All slashing cheekbones and liquid eyes, that creamy porcelain skin women's face cream ads always raved about. Her mouth was wide, with an alluringly full lower lip. At the moment, the face continued to frown.

"They had the address for billing," he continued. "Since I had a couple of hours, I thought I'd come by and check it out. Look, I can come back tomorrow, if you'd feel more comfortable. But I'm here now." He shrugged. "I can show you my press pass."

He pulled it out for her, and was

pleased when she narrowed her eyes to study it. "I do a column. J. Cooper McKinnon on sports. 'All in the Game'?"

"Oh." It meant nothing to her. The sports page wasn't her choice of reading material. But the smile had appeased her. He didn't look so much like a thug when he smiled. And the smear of paint decorating the lean, tanned face added just enough comedy to soothe her. "I guess it's all right, then. I wasn't expecting to show the apartment for a couple of days yet. It's not ready." She held up the can, set it down again. "I'm still painting."

"I noticed."

She laughed at that. It was a full-throated, smoky sound that went with the natural huskiness of her voice. "Guess you did. I'm Zoe Fleming." She crouched down to dampen a rag with paint remover.

"Thanks." He rubbed the rag over his cheek. "The ad said immediate occupancy."

"Well, I figured I'd be finished in here by tomorrow, when the ad was scheduled to run. Are you from the area?"

"I've got a place downtown. I'm looking for something with a little more space, a little more atmosphere."

"This is a pretty good-sized apartment. It was converted about eight years ago. The guy who owned it had it done for his son, and when he died, the son sold it and moved to California. He wanted to write sitcoms."

Coop walked over to check out the

view. He moved fluidly, Zoe thought, like a man who knew how to stay light and ready on his feet. She'd had the impression of wiry strength when her body tumbled into his. And good strong hands. Quick ones, too. She pursed her lips. It might be handy to have a man around.

"Is it just you, Mr. McKinnon?" She thought wistfully how nice it would be if he had a family — another child for Keenan to play with.

"Just me." The place felt right, he decided. It would be good to get out of a box that was just one more box in a building of boxes, to smell grass now and then. Barbecue smoke. "I can move in over the weekend."

She hadn't thought it would be so easy, and she nibbled her lip as she thought it through. She'd never been a landlady before, but she'd been a tenant, and she figured she knew the ropes. "I'll need first and last months' rent."

"Yeah."

"And, ah, references."

"I'll give you the number of the management company that handles my building. You can call Personnel at the paper. Have you got a lease for me to sign?"

She didn't. She'd checked out a book from the library, and she'd meant to type up a scaled-down copy of a lease from it the next morning. "I'll have it tomorrow. Don't you want to look at the rest of the apartment, ask any questions?" She'd been practicing her landlady routine for days.

"I've seen it. It's fine."

"Well." That deflated her a bit. "I guess I can cancel the ad."

There was a sound like a herd of rampaging elephants. Zoe glanced toward the open door and crouched to intercept the missile that hurtled through.

It was a boy, Coop saw when she scooped the child up. He had glossy golden hair, red sneakers, and jeans that were streaked with some unidentifiable substance that looked like it would easily transfer to other surfaces. He carried a plastic lunch box with a picture of some apocalyptic space battle on it, and a sheet of drawing paper that was grimy at the edges.

"I drew the ocean," he announced. "And a million people got ate by sharks."

"Gruesome." Zoe shuddered obligingly before accepting his sloppy kiss. She set him down to admire the drawing. "These are really big sharks," she said, cagily distinguishing the shark blobs from the people blobs.

"They're monster sharks. Mutant monster sharks. They have teeth."

"So I see. Keenan, this is Mr. Mc-Kinnon. Our new tenant."

Keenan wrapped one arm around Zoe's leg for security as he eyed the stranger. His eyes were working their way up to Coop's face when they lit on the T-shirt. "That's baseball. I'm gonna learn. Mama's getting a book so's she can teach me."

A book. Coop barely checked a snort. As if you could learn the greatest game invented by Man from a book. What kind of nerd did the kid have for a father?

"Great." It was all Coop intended to say. He'd always thought it wise to avoid entangling himself in a conversation with anyone under sixteen.

Keenan had other ideas. "If you're going to live here, you have to pay rent. Then we can pay the mortgage and stuff and go to Disney World."

What *was* the kid? An accountant?

"Okay, old man." Zoe laughed and ruffled his hair. "I can handle it from here. Go on down and put your stuff away."

"Is Beth coming to play with me tonight?"

"Yes, Beth's coming. Now scoot. I'll be down in a minute."

" 'Kay." He made a dash for the door, stopping when his mother called him. It only took one look, the raised brow for him to remember. He looked back at Coop, flashed a quick, sunny grin. "Bye, mister."

The herd of elephants rampaged again, then there was the crash of a door slamming. "He makes an entrance," Zoe said as she turned back to Coop. "The dramatic flair comes from my mother. She's an actress, off-off-Broadway." Tilting her head, Zoe rested one bare foot on the bottom rung of the stepladder. "You look like you're ready to change your mind. You have a problem with children?"

"No." The kid might have thrown him off, but Coop doubted it would be a problem. The boy would hardly be beating a path to his door. And if he did, Coop thought, he could send him off again quickly enough.

"No, he's, ah, cute."

"Yes, he is. I won't claim he's an angel, but he won't make a nuisance of himself. If he gives you any trouble, just let me know."

"Sure. Look, I'll come by tomorrow to sign the lease and give you a check. I'll pick up the keys then."

"That'll be fine."

"Any special time good for you?"

She looked blank for a moment. "What's tomorrow?"

"Friday."

"Friday." She closed her eyes and flipped through her messy internal calendar. "I'm working between ten and two. I think." She opened her eyes again, smiled. "Yeah, I'm pretty sure. Anytime after two-thirty?"

"Fine. Nice meeting you, Mrs. Fleming."

She took his offered hand. "It's Miss," she said easily. "I'm not married. And since we'll be living together, so to speak, you can make it Zoe."

Chapter 2

No one answered the door. Again. Coop checked his watch and saw that it was quarter to three. He didn't like to think he was a man obsessed with time, but as his living centered around deadlines, he did respect it. There was no rusting station wagon in the driveway this time, but he walked around the back of the house, hoping. Before he could start up the stairs to the apartment, he was hailed from across the chain-link fence.

"Young man! Yoo-hoo, young man!" Across the yard next door came a flowered muumuu, topped with a curling thatch of brightly hennaed hair that crowned a wide

29

face. The woman hurried to the fence in a whirl of color. It wasn't just the dress and the improbable hair, Coop noted. The face itself was a rainbow of rich red lipstick, pink cheeks and lavender eye shadow.

When she reached the fence, she pressed a many-ringed hand over the wide shelf of her breasts. "Not as young as I used to be," she said. "I'm Mrs. Finkleman."

"Hi."

"You're the young man who's going to live upstairs." Mrs. Finkleman, a born flirt, patted her curls. "Zoe didn't tell me you were so handsome. Single, are you?"

"Yeah," Coop said cautiously. "Miss Fleming was supposed to meet me. She doesn't seem to be home."

"Well, that's Zoe, flying here, flying

there." Mrs. Finkleman beamed and leaned comfortably on the fence, as if she were settling in for a nice cozy gossip. "Got a dozen things on her plate at once, that girl does. Having to raise that sweet little boy all alone. Why, I don't know what I'd have done without my Harry when our young ones were coming up."

Coop was a reporter, after all. That, added to the fact that he was curious about his landlady, put him in interview mode. "The kid's father doesn't help out any?"

Mrs. Finkleman snorted. "Don't see hide nor hair of him. From what I'm told, he lit out the minute he found out Zoe was expecting. Left her high and dry, and her hardly more than a child herself. Far as I know, he's never so much as seen the boy.

The little sweetheart."

Coop assumed she was referring to Keenan. "Nice kid. What's he, five, six?"

"Just four. Bright as a button. They grow them smarter these days. Teach them faster, too. The little love's in preschool now. He'll be home any minute."

"His mother went to pick him up, then?"

"Oh, no, not her week for car pool. Alice Miller — that's the white house with blue trim, down the block? — it's her week. She has a boy and a girl. Little darlings. The youngest, Steffie, is Keenan's age. Now her oldest, Brad, there's a pistol for you."

As she began to fill Coop in on the neighborhood rascal, he decided it was time to draw the interview to a close. "Maybe you could tell Miss Fleming I was by? I can leave a number where she can reach me when —"

"Oh, goodness." Mrs. Finkleman waved a hand. "I do run on. Nearly forgot why I came out here in the first place. Zoe called and asked me to look out for you. Got held up at the flower shop. She works there three days a week. That's Floral Bouquet, down in Ellicott City? Nice place, but expensive. Why, it's a crime to charge so much for a daisy."

"She got held up," Coop prompted.

"Her relief had car trouble, so Zoe's going to be a little late. Said you could go right on into the kitchen there, where she left the lease and the keys."

"That's fine. Thanks."

"No problem at all. This is a friendly neighborhood. Always somebody to lend a helping hand. I don't think Zoe mentioned what you did for a living."

"I'm a sportswriter for the *Dispatch.*"

"You don't say? Why, my Harry's just wild for sports. Can't budge him from in front of the TV when a game's on."

"That's what makes this country great."

Mrs. Finkleman laughed and gave Coop's arm an affectionate bat that might have felled a lesser man. "You men are all the same. You can come over and talk sports with Harry anytime. Me, if it's not baseball, it isn't worth talking about."

Coop, who'd been about to retreat, brightened. "You like baseball?"

"Son, I'm a Baltimore native." As if that said it all. "Our boys are going to go all the way this year. Mark my word."

"They could do it, if they heat those bats up. The pitching rotation's gold this year, and the infield's tight as a drum. What they need —"

Coop was interrupted by a cheerful toot. He glanced over to see Keenan burst out of a red sedan and rocket across the side yard.

"Hi, mister. Hi, Mrs. Finkleman. Carly Myers fell down, and there was blood." The big brown eyes gleamed wickedly. "Lots and lots of it, and she screamed and cried." He demon-strated, letting go with a piercing yell that had Coop's ears ringing. "Then

she got a Band-Aid with stars on it."
Keenan thought it would have been
worth losing some blood for such a
neat badge of honor. "Where's
Mama?"

"Little lamb." Mrs. Finkleman
leaned over the fence to pinch
Keenan's cheek. "She's working a
little late. She said you could come
stay with me until she gets home."

"Okay." Keenan liked his visits
next door, since they always included
cookies and a rock on Mrs.
Finkleman's wonderfully soft lap. "I
gotta put my lunch box away."

"Such a good boy," Mrs.
Finkleman cooed. "You come on
over when you're done. Why don't
you show the nice man inside so he
can wait for your mother?"

"Okay."

Before Coop could take evasive action, his hand was clutched by Keenan's. He'd been right, he thought with a wince. It was sticky.

"We've got cookies," Keenan told him, cannily deducing that he could have double his afternoon's treat if he played his cards right.

"Great."

"We baked them ourselves, on our night off." Keenan sent Coop a hopeful look. "They're really good."

"I bet." Coop caught the back door before it could slam shut.

"There." Keenan pointed to a ceramic cookie jar in the shape of a big yellow bird on the counter. "In Big Bird."

"Okay, okay." Since it seemed like the best way to appease the kid, Coop reached in and pulled out a handful of cookies. When he dumped them on the table, Keenan's eyes went as wide as saucers. He could hardly believe his luck.

"You can have one, too." He stuffed an entire chocolate chip deluxe in his mouth and grinned.

"That good, huh?" With a shrug, Coop sampled one himself. The kid, Coop decided after the first bite, knew his cookies. "You'd better get next door."

Keenan devoured another cookie, stalling. "I gotta wash out my thermos, 'cause if you don't, it smells."

"Right." Cooper sat at the table to read through the lease while the boy dragged a stool in front of the sink.

Keenan squirted dishwashing liquid in the thermos, and then, when he noticed Coop wasn't paying any attention, he squirted some more. And more. He turned the water up high and giggled when soap began to bubble and spew. With his tongue caught between his teeth, he jiggled the stopper into the sink and began to play dishwasher.

Coop forgot about him, reading quickly. The lease seemed standard enough, he decided. Zoe had already signed both copies. He dashed his signature across from hers, folded his copy, then set the check he'd already written on the table. He'd picked up the keys and rose to tuck his copy in his pocket when he spotted Keenan.

"Oh, God."

The boy was drenched, head to foot. Soap bubbles dotted his face and hair. A good-sized puddle was forming on the tile at the base of the stool.

"What are you doing?"

Keenan looked over his shoulder, smiled innocently. "Nothing."

"Look, you've got water everywhere." Coop looked around for a towel.

"Everywhere," Keenan agreed, and, testing the opposition, he slapped his hands in the sink. Water and suds geysered.

"Cut it out! Jeez! Aren't you supposed to be somewhere else?" He grabbed a dish towel and advanced, only to be slapped in the face by the next geyser. His eyes narrowed. "Look, kid —"

He heard the front door slam. Like mother, like son, he thought.

"Keenan?" Zoe called out. "I hope

you haven't been into those cookies."

Coop looked at the crumbs on the table, on the floor, floating in the soapy water.

"Oh, hell," he muttered.

"Oh, hell," Keenan echoed, beaming at him. He giggled and danced on his stool. "Hi, Mom."

Zoe, her arms full of day-old irises, took in the scene with one glance. Her son was as wet as a drowned dog, her kitchen looked as though a small hurricane had blown through. Hurricane Keenan, she thought. And her new tenant looked damp, frazzled, and charmingly sheepish.

Like a boy caught with his hand in the cookie jar, she noted, glancing at the telltale crumbs.

"Been playing dishwasher again?" With a calm that baffled Coop, she set the flowers down. "I'm just not sure it's the right career choice, Keen-man."

Keenan fluttered his long, wet lashes. "He wanted cookies."

Coop started to defend himself, then simply scowled at the boy.

"I'm sure he did. Go on into the laundry room and get out of those wet clothes."

"Okay." He jumped from the stool, splashing more water before he zoomed away. He stopped only long enough to give his mother a wet kiss before he disappeared into an adjoining room.

"Sorry I'm late," Zoe said easily, yanking the stopper out of the sink then walking to a cupboard to get a vase.

Coop opened his mouth. He

started to explain what had gone on in the past ten minutes, but realized he wasn't at all sure. "I signed the lease."

"I see that. Would you mind putting some water in this?" She held out the vase. "I need to get a mop."

"Sure."

She was probably going to wallop the kid with it, Coop thought, and felt a quick tug of regret and guilt. But the sounds from the laundry room where she'd disappeared weren't those he associated with corporal punishment. They were a young boy's giggles, a woman's lusty laugh. Coop stood, a vase of water in his hands, and wondered at it.

"You're standing in a puddle," Zoe commented when she came back with a mop and pail.

"Oh, right." Coop glanced down at his wet hightops, shifted. "Here's your vase."

"Thanks." She tended to her flowers first. "You met Mrs. Finkleman, I hear."

"News travels fast."

"Around here it does." When she handed him a dishcloth to dry his face with, he caught her scent — much more potent, much more colorful, than the flowers. She was wearing jeans and a baggy T-shirt with Floral Bouquet across the chest. Her hair, he noted, was some elusive shade between brown and blond. She wore it tied back in a jaunty ponytail.

When she lifted her brows, he realized he'd been staring. "Sorry. I mean — I'm sorry about the mess."

"Were you playing dishwasher, too?"

"Not exactly." It was impossible not to smile back, to ignore the quick pull of attraction.

It wouldn't be so bad, he mused, having a pretty landlady, sharing the house with her, maybe an occasional meal. Or an occasional —

"Mama!" Keenan stood in the doorway, wearing nothing but skin. "I can't find my pants."

"In the basket by the washing machine," she told him, without taking her eyes from Coop's.

He'd forgotten about the kid, let himself fantasize a little before remembering she didn't come as a single. He took a long mental step backward and jingled the keys to his new apartment.

"I've got some boxes out in the car," he told her. "I'm going to move some things in this afternoon."

"That's fine." It was silly to feel disappointed, Zoe thought. Foolish to have felt that fast feminine flutter when she recognized interest in his eyes. More foolish to feel let down because the interest had blanked out when her child called her. "Do you need any help?"

"No, I can handle it. I've got a game to cover tonight, so I'm going to move the rest in tomorrow." He backed toward the door. "Thanks."

"Welcome aboard, Mr. McKinnon."

"Coop," he said as he stepped outside. "It's Coop."

Coop, she thought, leaning on the mop handle. It had seemed like such a good idea to make use of the apartment upstairs. The extra income would take some of the pressure off, and maybe add a few bonuses. Like that trip to Disney World that Keenan wanted so badly.

It had been a risk to buy the house, but she'd wanted her son to grow up in a nice neighborhood, with a yard, maybe a dog when he was a little older. The rental income would take away some of the risk.

But she hadn't realized it could add another, more personal risk. She hadn't realized how awkward it might be to have a tenant who was male, single, and absolutely gorgeous.

She laughed at herself. Dream on, Zoe, she thought. J. Cooper Mc-Kinnon was just like the rest, who ran like a hound when they heard the patter of little feet.

Something crashed in the laundry

room. She just shook her head.

"Come on, sailor," she called to Keenan. "It's time to swab the deck."

Chapter 3

"Pretty good digs, Coop. Really, pretty good." Ben Robbins, a staff reporter for the *Dispatch*, sipped a cold one while surveying Coop's apartment. "I didn't think much of it when we hauled all your junk up here, but it ain't half-bad."

It was a lot better than not half-bad, and Coop knew it. He had everything exactly where he wanted it. The living room was dominated by his long, low-slung sofa of burgundy leather and his big-screen television, so perfect for viewing games. A couple of brass lamps, a nicely worn coffee table scuffed from the heels of the dozens of shoes that had rested on it and a single generous chair completed the formal section of the room.

There was an indoor basketball hoop, small-scaled, for practice — and because shooting a little round ball helped him think. A used pinball machine called Home Run, a stand that held two baseball bats, his tennis racket and a hockey stick, a pair of old boxing gloves hanging on the wall and a scarred Fooz Ball table made up the recreation area.

Coop wouldn't have called them toys. They were tools.

He'd chosen blinds, rather than curtains, for the windows. Blinds, he thought, that would close out the light if a man decided to treat himself to an afternoon nap.

The bedroom held little other than his bed, a nightstand and another

TV. The room was for sleeping — or, if he got lucky, another type of sport.

But it was his office that pleased him most. He could already imagine himself spending hours there at his computer, a game playing on his desktop TV. He'd outfitted it with a big swivel chair, a desk that had just the right number of scars and burns, a fax, a dual-line phone and a VCR — to play back those controversial calls or heart-stopping plays.

With all the plaques and photos and sports memorabilia scattered about, it was home.

His home.

"Looks like the neighborhood bar," Ben said, and stretched out his short, hairy legs. "Where the jocks hang out."

Coop considered that the highest of

compliments. "It suits me."

"To the ground," Ben agreed, and toasted Coop with his bottle of beer. "A place where a man can relax, be himself. You know, since I started living with Sheila, I've got little china things all over, and underwear hanging in the bathroom. The other day she comes home with a new bedspread. It's got *flowers* all over. Pink flowers." He winced as he drank. "It's like sleeping in a meadow."

"Hey." With all the smug righteousness of the unencumbered, Coop propped his feet on the coffee table. "Your choice, pal."

"Yeah, yeah. Too bad I'm nuts about her. And her an Oakland fan, too."

"Takes all kinds. Talk is the A's are trading Remirez."

Ben snorted. "Yeah, yeah, pull the other one, champ."

"That's the buzz." Coop shrugged, took a pull on his own beer. "Sending him to K.C. for Dunbar, and that rookie fielder, Jackson."

"They got to be crazy. Remirez hit .280 last season."

".285," Coop told him. "With twenty-four baggers. Led the team in errors, too."

"Yeah, but with a bat like that . . . And Dunbar, what's he? Maybe he hit .220?"

"It was .218, but he's like a vacuum cleaner at second. Nothing gets by him. And the kid's got potential. Big, strapping farm boy with an arm like a bullet. They need new blood. Most of the starting lineup's over thirty."

They argued baseball and finished

their beers in complete male harmony.

"I've got a game to cover."

"Tonight? I thought the O's were in Chicago until tomorrow."

"They are." Coop pocketed his tape recorder, his pad, a pencil. "I'm covering the college game. There's a hot third baseman who's got the scouts drooling. Thought I'd take a look, cop an interview."

"What a job." Ben hauled himself to his feet. "Going to games, hanging around locker rooms."

"Yeah, it's a rough life." He slung an arm over Ben's shoulders as they headed out. "So, how's the story on neutering pets going?"

"Stuff it, Coop."

"Hey, some of us hang around the pound, some of us hang around the ballpark."

And a hell of a day it was for it, too, Coop thought. Balmy and clear-skied. He could almost smell roasting peanuts and hot dogs.

"While you're hanging around a bunch of sweaty college boys in jock-straps, I'll be snuggled up with a woman."

"Under a flowered bedspread."

"Yeah, but she says flowers make her feel sexy. And I'm here to tell you — My, oh, my . . ."

When Ben's small, square face went lax, Coop turned. He felt his own jaw drop. And, if he wasn't mis-taken, his tongue landed on his shoes.

She was wearing what had to be the shortest skirt ever devised by man. Beneath it were a pair of endless legs that were molded into black fishnet hose. She swayed when she walked.

How could she help it, when she stood in black skyscraper heels?

A tiny white bustier exposed a delicious amount of cleavage. Around her neck was a shiny black bow tie that, for reasons utterly inexplicable to Coop, made every male cell in his body sizzle.

Her hair was down, falling straight as a pin to her shoulders in a melding of tones that made him think of wild deer leaping through a sunlit forest.

She stopped, smiled, said something, but his mind had checked out the moment his eyes landed on her legs.

". . . if you've settled in okay."

"Ah . . ." He blinked like a man coming out of a coma. "What?"

"I said I haven't had a chance to

check and see if you've settled in okay."

"Fine." He folded his tongue back in his mouth and got a grip on himself. "Just fine."

"Good. Keenan came down with a cold, so things have been hectic. I caught a glimpse of you hauling things up the steps a couple of days ago."

"Hauling," he repeated. "Yeah. Ben," he said when his friend jabbed him. "This is Ben. He's been giving me a hand moving."

"Hi, Ben. I'm Zoe."

"Hi, Zoe," Ben said stupidly. "I'm Ben."

She just smiled. It was the outfit, she knew. As much as she hated it, she couldn't help but be amused by how it affected certain members of the species. "Do you work at the paper, too?"

"Yeah, I'm, ah, doing a story on neutering pets."

"Really?" She almost felt sorry for him, the way his Adam's apple was bobbing. "I'll be sure to look for it. I'm glad you're settling in okay. I've got to get to work."

"You're going out?" Coop said. "In that?"

Her lips twitched. "Well, this is my usual outfit when I'm carpooling, but I thought I'd wear it to work tonight. At Shadows? I'm a waitress. Nice meeting you, Ben."

She walked to her car. No, Coop thought, swayed to it, in those long, lazy strides. They were both still staring when she pulled out of the drive and cruised down the street.

"Your landlady," Ben said in a reverential whisper. "That was your landlady."

"I think it was." She hadn't looked like that when he signed the lease. Beautiful, yes — she'd been beautiful, but in a wholesome, unthreatening sort of way. She hadn't looked so . . . so . . . Words failed him. She was a mother, for God's sake, he reminded himself. She wasn't supposed to look like that. "She's got a kid."

"Yeah? What kind?"

"Human, I think."

"Come on."

"A boy," Coop said absently. "This high." He held a hand, palm down, about three feet from the ground.

"She may have a kid, but she's also got legs. This high." Ben waved a hand in front of his own throat. "You got a charmed life, Coop. My landlord's got arms like cinder blocks, and a tattoo of a lizard. You got one who looks like a centerfold."

"She's a mother," Coop said under his breath.

"Well, I wouldn't mind coming home to her for milk and cookies. See you at the sweatshop."

"Sure." Coop stood where he was, frowning at the quiet street. Mothers weren't supposed to look like that, he thought again. They were supposed to look . . . motherly. Safe. Comfortable. He blew out a breath, willed away the knot in his stomach.

She wasn't *his* mother, he reminded himself.

By midnight, Zoe's feet were

screaming. Her back ached, and her arms felt as though she'd been hauling boulders rather than drink trays. She'd deflected six propositions, two of them good-hearted enough to amuse, one of them insulting enough to earn the gentleman in question a bruised instep, courtesy of one of her stiletto heels. The others had been the usual, and easily ignored.

It went with the territory, and it didn't bother her overmuch.

The lounge earned its name from the shadowy effect of neon and all the dim corners. The decor was fifties tacky, and the waitresses were dolled up like old-fashioned mindless floozies to match.

But the tips were excellent, and the clientele, for the most part, harmless.

"Two house wines, white, a Black Russian and a coffee, light." After calling out her order to the bartender, Zoe took a moment to roll her shoulders.

She hoped Beth had gotten Keenan to bed without any fuss. He'd been cranky all day — which meant he was nearly over his sniffles. He'd put up quite a fuss that morning, Zoe remembered, when she'd nixed the idea of him going to school.

Didn't get that from me, she thought. She'd never fussed about not going to school. Now, at twenty-five, she deeply regretted letting her education slide. If she'd applied herself, tried for college, she could have developed a skill, had a career.

Instead, she had a high school diploma she'd barely earned, and was qualified for little more than serving drinks to men whose eyes tried to crawl down her cleavage.

But she wasn't one for regrets. She'd done what she'd done, and she had the greatest prize of all. Keenan. In a couple of years, she figured, she'd have saved enough that she could turn in her bustier and take a night course. Once she had a few business courses under her belt, she could open her own flower shop. And she wouldn't have to leave Keenan with sitters at night.

She served her drinks, took an order from another table and thanked God her break was coming up in five minutes.

When she saw Coop walk in, her first thought was Keenan. But the sick alarm passed almost as quickly as it had come. Coop was relaxed, obviously scoping the place out. When his eyes met hers, he nodded easily and made his way through the scattered tables.

"I thought I'd stop in for a drink."

"This is the place for it. Do you want to sit at the bar, or do you want a table?"

"A table. Got a minute?"

"At quarter after I've got fifteen of them. Why?"

"I'd like to talk to you."

"Okay. What can I get you?"

"Coffee, black."

"Coffee, black. Have a seat."

He watched her head toward the bar and tried not to dwell on how attractive she looked walking away. He hadn't come in because he wanted a drink, but because she seemed like a nice woman in a tight skirt — spot, he corrected. A tight spot.

Get hold of yourself, Coop, he warned himself. He knew better than to let a pair of long legs cloud his judgment. He'd only come in to ask a few questions, get the full story. That was what he did, and he was good at it. Just as he was good at dissecting a game, any game, and finding those small triumphs and small mistakes that influenced the outcome.

"We've been busy tonight." Zoe set two coffees on the table before sliding onto a chair across from Coop. She let out a long, heartfelt sigh, then smiled. "This is the first time I've been off my feet in four hours."

"I thought you worked in a flower shop."

"I do, three days a week." She slid

her cramped feet out of her shoes. "Around Mother's Day, Christmas, Easter — you know, the big flower days, I can squeeze in more." She sipped the coffee she'd loaded with sugar and let it pump into her system. "It's just a small shop, and Fred — that's the owner — only keeps on a couple of part-timers. That way he doesn't have to pay any of the bennies, like hospitalization, sick leave."

"That's lousy."

"Hey, it's a job. I like it. It's just Fred and Martha — she's his wife. They've taught me a lot about flowers and plants."

Someone pumped quarters into the juke. The room heated up with music. Coop leaned over the table so that she could hear him. For a moment he lost the thread somewhere in her big brown eyes.

"Have I met you somewhere before?" he asked her.

"In the apartment."

"No, I mean . . ." He shook his head, let it go. "Uh, why here?"

"Why here what?"

"Why do you work here?"

She blinked, those long lashes fluttering down, then up. "For a paycheck."

"It doesn't seem like you should be working in a bar."

"Excuse me?" Zoe wasn't sure if she should be amused or insulted. She chose the former simply because it was her nature. "Do you have a problem with cocktail waitresses?"

"No, no. It's just that, you're a mother."

"Yes, I am. I have a son to prove it."

She laughed and leaned her chin on her fist. "Are you thinking it would be more appropriate for me to be home baking cookies or knitting a scarf?"

"No." Though it embarrassed him that he did. "It's that outfit," he blurted out. "And the way all these men look at you."

"If a woman's going to wear something like this, men are going to look. Looking's all they do," she added. "If it makes you feel better, I don't dress like this for PTA meetings."

He was feeling more ridiculous every second. "Look, it's none of my business. I just have a habit of asking questions. Seems to me you could do better than this. I mean, you've got the flower job, and the rent —"

"And I have a mortgage, a son who seems to outgrow his clothes and shoes every other week, a car payment, grocery bills, doctor bills."

"Doctor? Is the kid sick?"

Zoe rolled her eyes. Just when she was starting to get irritated, he deflated her. "No. Kids Keenan's age are always bringing some germ or other home from school. He needs regular checkups with his pediatrician, with the dentist. Those things aren't free."

"No, but there are programs. Assistance." He stopped, because those big brown eyes had turned fierce.

"I'm perfectly capable of earning a living, and of taking care of my child."

"I didn't mean —"

"Maybe I don't have a college degree or any fancy skills, but I can pay my own way, and my son doesn't lack for anything." She jammed her feet into the backbreaking heels and stood. "We've been doing just fine on our own, and I don't need some nosy jock reporter coming in here and telling me how to be a mother. Coffee's on the house, you jerk."

He winced as she stormed away from the table, then let out a long breath. Handled that one *real* well, Coop.

He wondered if there would be an eviction notice on his door in the morning.

Chapter 4

She didn't kick him out. She had thought of it, but had decided the satisfaction she'd gain didn't quite equal the rental income. Besides, she'd heard it all before.

One of the reasons she'd moved from New York was that she'd grown impossibly weary of friends and family telling her how to run her life. How to raise her son.

Baltimore had been a clean slate.

She'd had enough money put aside to afford a nice two-bedroom apartment and invest the rest. And because she was willing to work at any job, and work hard, she'd rarely been unemployed. It had been difficult for her to put Keenan in day-care. But he'd thrived. He had his mother's knack for making friends.

Now, two years after the move, she had a house, and a yard, in the kind of neighborhood she wanted for her son. And she'd paid for every bit of it on her own.

Too many people had told her she was crazy, that she was too young, that she was throwing her life and her chances away. With a grunt, Zoe shoved the lawn mower around and began to cut another strip of grass. *Her* grass, she thought with clenched teeth.

She'd proved them wrong. She'd had her baby, kept her baby, and she was making a decent life for him. She and Keenan weren't statistics. They were a family.

They didn't need anyone to feel sorry for them, or to offer handouts. She was taking care of everything, one step at a time. And she had plans. Good, solid plans.

The tap on her shoulder made her jump. When she whipped her head around and looked at Coop, her hands tightened on the mower. "What?"

"I want to apologize," he shouted. When she only continued to glare at him, he reached down and shut off the engine. "I want to apologize," he repeated. "I was out of line last night."

"Really?"

"I'm sort of addicted to poking into other people's business."

"Maybe you should go cold turkey." She reached down to grab

the pull cord. His hand closed over hers. She stared at it a moment. He had big hands, rough-palmed. She remembered the impression she'd gotten of strength and energy. Now the hand was gentle and hard to resist.

She hadn't felt a man's hands — hadn't wanted to feel a man's hands — in a very long time.

"Sometimes I push the wrong buttons," Coop continued. He was staring at their hands, as well, thinking how small hers felt under his. How soft. "It's earned me a fist in the face a time or two." He tried a smile when her gaze slid up to his.

"That doesn't surprise me."

She didn't smile back, but he sensed a softening. The roar of the mower had awakened him. When he'd looked out and seen her marching along behind it in baggy shorts, a T-shirt and a ridiculous straw hat, he'd wanted to go back to bed. But he'd been compelled to seek her out.

It was only a flag of truce, he told himself. After all, he had to live with her. More or less.

"I didn't mean to be critical. I was curious about you. And the kid," he added quickly. "And maybe seeing you in that outfit last night pushed a few of my buttons."

She lifted a brow. That was honest enough, she thought. "All right. No permanent damage."

It had been easier than he'd expected. Coop decided to press his luck. "Listen, I've got to cover the game this afternoon. Maybe you'd like to come along. It's a nice day for baseball."

She supposed it was. It was warm and sunny, with a nice, freshening breeze. There were worse ways to spend the day than in a ballpark with an attractive man who was doing his best to pry his foot out of his mouth.

"It sounds like fun — if I didn't have to work. But Keenan would love it." She watched his jaw drop, and smothered a smile.

"Keenan? You want me to take him?"

"I can't think of anything he'd rather do. Some of the kids play in their yards, and they let him chase the ball. But he's never seen the real thing, except on TV." She smiled now, guilelessly, and held back a hoot of laughter. She could all but see

76

Coop's mind working.

"I don't know too much about kids," he said, backpedaling cautiously.

"But you know about sports. It'll be great for Keenan to experience his first real game with an expert. When are you leaving?"

"Ah . . . a couple of hours."

"I'll make sure he's ready. This is awfully nice of you." While he stood staring, she leaned over and kissed his cheek. After one hard tug, she had the mower roaring again.

Coop stood planted like a tree when she strolled away. What the hell was he supposed to do with a kid all afternoon?

He bought popcorn, hot dogs and enormous cups of soft drinks. Coop figured food would keep the kid quiet. Keenan had bounced on the seat of the car throughout the drive to Camden Yards, and since they had arrived he'd goggled at everything.

Coop had heard "What's that?" and "How come?" too many times to count. Nervous as a cat, he settled into the press box with his laptop.

"You can watch through the window here," he instructed Keenan. "And you can't bother anybody, because they're working."

"Okay." Almost bursting with excitement, Keenan clutched his hot dog.

There were lots of people in the press box, some with neat computers, like Coop, others with headphones. A few of them had smiled at him, and all of them had said hello to Coop.

Keenan knew Coop was important. As his mother had instructed, he kept close and didn't ask for any presents. Even though there had been really neat stuff at the stands. His mother had given him five whole dollars and told him he could buy a souvenir. But there'd been so many he didn't know which to pick. And Coop had walked so fast he'd hardly been able to look.

But it didn't matter, because he was at a real ball game.

Wide-eyed, he stared down at the field. It was bigger than anything he'd imagined. He knew where the pitcher would stand, and he recognized home plate, but he wasn't sure of anything else.

The big scoreboard exploded with pictures, and words he couldn't read. Circling it all were the stands, filled

79

with more people than he'd ever seen.

When they announced the lineup, he looked down at the players with naked admiration. The national anthem began, and, recognizing it, Keenan stood up, as he'd been taught.

Coop glanced over, saw the boy standing, with a hot dog in one hand and a big, dazzling grin on his face. Suddenly he remembered his first time at a ballpark. His eager hand gripping his father's, his eyes trying to see everything at once, and his heart so full of the excitement, of the game, of just being a boy.

As the players took the field, Coop reached over and tugged on Keenan's bright hair. "Pretty cool, huh?"

"It's the best ever. Those are our guys, right?"

"Those are our guys. They're gonna kick butt."

Keenan giggled and leaned closer to the glass to watch the first pitch. "Kick butt," he said with relish.

He didn't, as Coop had expected, fidget, whine or make a general nuisance of himself. Because he was accustomed to working under noisy and confusing conditions, Keenan's constant questions didn't annoy him overmuch. At least, he thought, the kid had the good sense to ask.

Between innings, Keenan peered over Coop's shoulder and sounded out the words that were popping up on the computer screen, and he did transfer some mustard from his hands onto Coop's sleeve. But it wasn't the disaster Coop had envisioned.

Coop even felt a quick tug of pride when the play-by-play announcer called Keenan over and let the boy sit in his lap for an inning.

Most kids would've been running around the booth begging for more candy. But this one, Coop thought, had come for the game.

"How come he didn't run all the way? How come he didn't?" Keenan shifted from foot to foot. His bladder was past full, but he couldn't bear to miss a minute.

"The throw went to second, so he was forced out," Coop explained. "See, the second baseman caught the ball and stepped on the bag to retire the side."

"Retire the side," Keenan repeated reverently. "But we're still winning?"

"The O's are up by one going into

the top of the ninth. Looking at the batting order, I'd say they'll put in a southpaw."

"Southpaw," Keenan repeated, as if it were gospel.

"A left-handed reliever. Probably Scully." He glanced over and noted that Keenan was holding his crotch. "Uh, got a problem?"

"Nuh-uh."

"Let's hit the john — the bath-room." He took Keenan's hand and hoped it wasn't too late. As they passed through the door, Scully was announced as the relief.

"Just like you said." Keenan looked up at Coop with dazzling admiration. "You're smarter than anybody."

Coop felt a grin break out over his face. "Let's just say I know the game."

★ ★ ★

When they arrived home, Keenan was wearing a new Orioles jersey and carrying an autographed baseball in a pint-size baseball glove. He waved a pennant in his other hand as he scrambled up the steps.

"Look! Look what Coop got me!" He barreled into his mother who'd barely walked in the door herself. "We went into the locker room with the real Orioles, and they signed the baseball for me. To keep."

"Let's see." She took the ball and examined it. "This is really special, Keenan."

"I'm gonna keep it forever. And I got this shirt, too, like they wear. And a glove. It even fits."

Emotion backed up in her throat. "It certainly does. Looks like you're all ready to play ball."

"I'm gonna play third base, 'cause it's the . . . the . . ."

"Hot corner," Coop supplied.

"Yeah. Can I go show Mr. Finkleman? Can I show him my baseball?"

"Sure."

"He's gonna be surprised." He turned and threw his arms around Coop's legs. "Thanks, thanks for taking me. I liked it best of anything. Can we go again, and take Mama?"

"Uh, yeah, I guess. Sure." Feeling awkward again, he patted Keenan's head.

"Okay!" Giving Coop one last squeeze, Keenan raced out the door to show off his treasures.

"You didn't have to buy him all that stuff," Zoe began. "Taking him was enough."

"No big deal. He didn't ask for it, or anything." Coop stuck his hands in his pockets. "He got such a charge out of meeting the players, and one thing kind of led to another."

"I know. I hear our team won."

"Yeah. Clipped them by one. I had to stop by the paper and file the story, or we'd have been here sooner."

"I just got in myself." On impulse, she walked over, wrapped her arms around him and hugged. Coop's hands stayed paralyzed in his pockets. "I owe you. You gave him a great day. He won't forget it." She drew back. "Neither will I."

"It's no big deal. He just hung out in the press box."

"It's a very big deal, especially since I trapped you into it." She laughed and tossed back her hair. "You were so transparent this morning, Coop. The idea of having a four-year-old tagging along terrified you. But you did good, real good. Anyway — Sorry," she said when the phone rang. "Hello? Oh, hi, Stan. Tonight? I'm not scheduled." Letting out a breath, she sat on the arm of a chair. "I'll have to let you know. No, Stan, I can't tell you now. I have to see if I can find a sitter. An hour, then. Yes, I understand you're in a jam. I'll call you back."

"Problem?"

"Hmmm . . . Two of the waitresses called in sick for tonight. They're short-staffed." She was already dialing the phone. "Hi, Mrs. Finkleman. Yeah, I know. He had a great time. Mm-hmm . . ." Zoe's gaze flicked up to Coop as Mrs. Finkleman told her how important it was for a boy to have a man in his life. "I'm sure you're right. I was wondering if you're busy tonight. Oh. That's right, I forgot. No, it's nothing. Have a good time."

Zoe hung up and pursed her lips. "It's their bingo night," she told Coop. "Beth's got a date. Maybe Alice." She reached for the phone again, shook her head. "No, she's having her in-laws over for dinner." Her eyes lit on Coop and narrowed in speculation. "You didn't have any problem with Keenan today."

"No," Coop said slowly, wary of another trap. "He was cool."

"Stan doesn't need me in until nine. Keenan goes to bed at eight, so you wouldn't have to do anything but hang around, watch television or whatever."

"Hang around here, while you

work?" He took a step back. "Just me and the kid — like a baby-sitter? Listen . . ."

"I'll pay you. Beth gets two an hour, but I can up the ante."

"I don't want your money, Zoe."

"That's so sweet." She smiled, took his hand and squeezed. "Really, so sweet of you. If you could come down about eight-thirty."

"I never said —"

"You can help yourself to anything in the kitchen. I'll make some brownies, if I have time. I'd better call Stan back before he pulls out what's left of his hair." She picked up the phone, beamed at Coop. "Now I owe you two."

"Yeah, right." He hurried out before she could find some way to owe him three.

Chapter 5

For the next couple of hours, Coop immersed himself in "All in the Game," his weekly syndicated column. The kid had given him the hook, he thought. The first visit to a ball game, the passing on of tradition, and the bond that was forged over the cheers, the crack of the bat, the peanut shells.

It was a good piece, Coop decided, and wrote easily. He supposed since he owed the idea to Keenan the least he could do was hang around downstairs and eat brownies while the kid slept.

He wandered back down just as Zoe came through the kitchen door.

She hadn't been sure he'd come.

She knew she'd hustled him, and after she'd finished being amused by it, she felt guilty. But here he was, right on time, standing at the foot of the steps.

"I pushed you into a corner. . . ." she began.

"Yeah, you did." She looked so somber, he had to smile. "You've got a real talent for it."

She shrugged her shoulders and smiled back at him. "Sometimes being pushy's the only way to get things done, but I always feel bad about it after. I did bake brownies."

"I could smell them all the way upstairs." When she didn't move, he tilted his head. Funny, though she was wearing that sexy waitress rig again, she didn't seem so outrageous. Except for that bow tie, he thought.

Something about that black tie around that slim white throat shot straight to his libido.

"You going to let me in, or do you want me to stand out here?"

"I have this guilt thing," she explained, "whenever I have to ask anyone for a favor. And it was so sweet of you to take Keenan to the game, especially when . . ."

"When I'd been asking you out?"

She shrugged her shoulders again, let them fall. He was looking at her that way again, and something in her body was reacting helplessly. Better, she thought, to set the rules quickly. "I don't go out with men. I should have told you straight out."

He had to force himself not to lift a hand to that neat little bow and tug. "At all?"

"It's just easier not to. They're not interested in Keenan, or they pretend they are so they can talk me into bed." When he rocked back on his heels and cleared his throat, she laughed. "What they don't know is that they're clear as cellophane. You see, Keenan and I are a team. As a sportswriter, you should know what that means."

"Sure. I get it."

"Anyway, you gave him a really wonderful day, and I feel like I'm twisting your arm about tonight."

He decided, after a moment, that she wasn't doing it on purpose. There was just too much sincerity in that glorious face for a con. And if there was a twinge of guilt because he had given considerable thought to talking her into bed, that was his problem.

"Look, he's asleep, right?"

"Yes. All the excitement wore him out."

"So, I'll eat your brownies and watch your TV. No big deal."

Her smile came easily now, beautifully, and made his mouth water. "I left the number of the club by the phone, just in case. The Finklemans should be home by eleven. She'd come over and relieve you if you want."

"We'll play it by ear."

"Thanks, really." She stepped back into the kitchen to let him in. "My shift ends at two, at closing."

"Long day for you."

"I've got tomorrow off." After grabbing her purse, she took a quick look around. "Make yourself at home, okay?"

"I will. See you."

She hurried out, those incredibly sexy heels clicking across the tile. Coop let out a long breath and told himself to settle down. The lady had just set the ground rules. Fun and games were out.

She had the face of a siren, the body of a goddess, and legs designed to make a strong man whimper — but deep in her heart she was Betty Crocker.

Coop took a deep sniff and decided to content himself with a plate of double fudge brownies.

The storm rolled in just before midnight. Coop had taken Zoe at her word and made himself at home. He was stretched out on her couch, sunk deep in the cushions, with his feet propped comfortably on her coffee table. He was dozing in front of an old war movie, his only regret being that he hadn't thought to bring a couple of beers down with him.

Zoe's selection ran to milk, juice and some unidentified green liquid.

He'd poked around a little — it was simply in his nature. The clutter ran throughout the house, but he began to see a pattern to it. Obviously she wasn't a detail person, but the general lack of order made the house comfortable, even cozy. Coop wasn't sure if the result was by design or simply because she was a woman who worked two jobs and had a kid to raise.

And from the library books he'd found stacked here and there, it seemed she spent most of her free time reading up on flowers, car repair, tax laws and time management.

He couldn't help but think it was a waste of a perfectly stunning woman, this voluntary burial of self in books and nowhere part-time jobs.

But it wasn't his problem.

The crash of thunder from outside harmonized nicely with the artillery barrage on the TV screen. Coop had just decided that this baby-sitting racket was a snap.

Then he heard the wailing.

Marines didn't wail, he thought fuzzily, especially when they were battling Nazi scum. He yawned, circled his neck until it cracked, then spotted Keenan.

The boy stood at the base of the stairs in Batman pajamas, a battered stuffed dog clutched in one arm and tears pouring down his face.

"Mama!" His voice sharpened like an ice pick, then hitched. "Where's my mama?"

"She's at work." Coop straightened on the sofa and stared helplessly. "Something wrong?"

A flash of lightning lit the room. By the time the thunder rolled in answer, Keenan screamed like a banshee and launched himself into Coop's lap.

"I'm scared. There's monsters outside. They're coming to get me."

"Hey . . ." Coop gave the head buried in his chest an inadequate pat. "Hey, it's just a thunderstorm."

"Monsters," Keenan sobbed. "I want Mama."

"Well, she's —" He started to swear, caught himself. The poor kid was shaking. With an instinct he didn't recognize, Coop cuddled Keenan in his lap. "You don't like storms, huh?" All Keenan could do was shake his head and burrow deeper. "They're just like fireworks. You know, on the Fourth of July, or after your team wins the pennant? They probably just had a big game up there. They're celebrating."

"Monsters," Keenan repeated, but he'd calmed enough to lift his head and look at Coop. "Big black monsters with sharp teeth." He jolted at the next clap of thunder. Fresh tears started to roll. "They want to eat me."

"Nah." Experimentally, Coop tested Keenan's biceps. "You're too tough."

"I am?"

"You bet. Any monsters who

looked in here would see you and run for their lives. They'd never take on Coop and the Keen-man."

Keenan sniffled, rubbed a fist over his eyes. "Really?"

"Absolutely." Coop saw Keenan's lower lip tremble when thunder grumbled. "Home run," he said, and Keenan's trembling mouth curved in a hesitant smile.

"Can I stay out here with you?"

"Sure. I guess."

Keenan, an expert in such matters, settled himself comfortably in Coop's lap, laid his head against Coop's heart and sighed.

Zoe was swaying with fatigue by the time she let herself in. It was nearly 3:00 a.m., and she'd been up and going for twenty hours straight. All she wanted was to fall facedown on her bed and sleep.

She saw them in the gray light of the snowy television screen. They were curled together on the couch, the boy snuggled deep against the man. Something shifted inside her at the sight of them, both sleeping deeply, Keenan's tousled golden hair beneath Coop's broad, tanned hand.

She set her purse and her keys aside without taking her eyes off them.

How small her son looked, and how safe.

She slipped out of her shoes and walked to them on stockinged feet. In a natural gesture, she brushed a hand over Coop's hair before gently lifting her son. Keenan stirred, then settled against her.

"Mama."

"Yes, baby," she murmured. She nuzzled him as she carried him away, caught the scent of man mixed with boy.

"The monsters came, but we scared them away."

"Of course you did."

"Coop said the thunder's just fireworks. I like fireworks."

"I know." She laid him in his bed, smoothing the sheets, his hair, kissing his soft cheeks. "Go back to sleep now."

But he already had. She watched him a moment longer in the faint glow of his night-light, then turned and went back downstairs to Coop.

He was sitting up now, his head in his hands, the heels rubbing against his eyes. She switched off the buzzing television set, then sat on the arm of the couch. Any man who could sleep so comfortably with a child, to her mind, had unlimited potential.

She wondered, just for an instant, what it would feel like to curl up beside him.

"The storm woke him?"

"Yeah." His voice was rusty. He cleared it. "He was pretty spooked."

"He said you chased the monsters away."

"Seemed like the right thing to do." He turned his head to look at her. Those big brown eyes were sleepy and smiling. The quick hitch in his heartbeat warned him to be on his way. But he lingered. "He's okay now?"

"He's fine. You'd make a good daddy."

"Oh, well . . ." That had him

moving. He stood, working out the kinks. "That's not my line. But it was no big deal."

"It was to me." She'd embarrassed him, she noted, and she hadn't meant to. "Why don't I fix you breakfast tomorrow?"

"Huh?"

"Pay you back with pancakes. Mrs. Finkleman tells me you bring in a lot of pizza and Chinese, so I don't imagine you cook. Do you like pancakes?"

"Who doesn't?"

"Then let me know when you're up and around. I'll flip some for you." She lifted a hand, brushed the hair from his brow. "Thanks for helping me out."

"No problem." He took a step away, swore under his breath and turned back. "Listen, I've just got to do this, okay?"

Before she could respond, he took her face in his hands and closed his mouth over hers.

The kiss was quick, and it was light, and it sent sparks snapping down her nerve ends.

When she didn't move a muscle, he lifted his head, looked at her. She was staring at him, her eyes heavy and dark. He thought he saw the same stunned reaction in them that was curling somewhere in his gut. She opened her mouth as if to speak, but he shook his head and kissed her again. Longer, deeper, until he felt her bones begin to melt. Until he heard the small whimper of pleasure purr in her throat.

Her hands slid up his arms,

gripped, then moved up to tangle in his hair. They stood there, locked against each other.

One of them quivered, perhaps both. It didn't seem to matter as the warm taste of her seeped into his mouth, into his blood. It was like a dream that he hadn't yet shaken off, one that tempted him to sink back in, to forget reality.

She'd forgotten it. All she knew for one glorious moment was that she was being held in strong arms, that her mouth was being savored wonderfully, and that needs, so long dormant, were swimming to the surface and breaking into life.

Touch me. She wondered if she said it, or if the words simply whirled hazily in her head. But his hand, hard and sure, ran once down her body, kindling fires.

She remembered what it was to burn, and what it was like when the flames died out and left you alone.

"Coop." Oh, she wanted, so badly, just to let it happen. But she wasn't a young, reckless girl this time. And she had more to think of than herself. "Coop. No."

His mouth clung to hers for another moment, his teeth nipping. But he drew back. He was, he realized, as breathless as a man who'd slid headfirst into home plate.

"Now I'm supposed to say I'm sorry."

She shook her head. "No, you're not. I'm not."

"Good." The hands that were resting on her shoulders kneaded once, then slipped away into his pockets. "Me neither. I've been thinking about doing that since I first saw your feet."

Her brows rose. Surely she'd heard him wrong. "My what?"

"Your feet. You were standing on the ladder, painting. You weren't wearing any shoes. You've got tremendously sexy feet."

"Really?" It amazed her that he could tie her into helpless knots one minute, then make her laugh the next. "Thanks. I think."

"I guess I'd better go."

"Yeah, you'd better."

He nodded, started out. This time, when he stopped, she braced, and she yearned. But he simply turned and looked at her. "I'm not going to try to talk you into bed. But I want you there. I figured I should let you know."

"I appreciate it," she said in a shaky voice.

When the door closed behind him, she let her weak legs fold and sat down on the couch. What, she asked herself, was she supposed to do now?

Chapter 6

When Coop dragged himself out of bed, it was nearly noon. He stumbled into the shower and nearly drowned himself before both of his eyes opened. Wet and out of sorts, he rubbed himself down, gave a moment's thought to shaving, then dismissed the idea.

He tugged on gym shorts and a T-shirt before heading directly to the coffeemaker. While it brewed, he opened his front door and let the full power of the sun shock him the rest of the way awake.

They were in the yard, Zoe and Keenan, laughing as mother tried to help son hit fungoes with a plastic bat. The kid wasn't having much luck, Coop noted. But he was sure having fun. He started to step back inside before either of them spotted him. But the jock in him had him kibitzing.

"He'll never hit anything standing that way," Coop called out, and had two pair of big brown eyes looking up in his direction.

"Hi, Coop. Hi. I'm playing baseball." Thrilled to have an audience, Keenan waved his bat and nearly caught his mother on the chin.

"Watch it, champ," she said, and shifted out of range. "Good morning," she called out. "Want your breakfast?"

"Yeah, maybe."

Keenan took another pathetic swing and had Coop muttering under

his breath. Swung like a girl. Somebody had to show the kid how to hold
a bat, didn't they? he asked himself as
he started down.

"You're choking it too much."

Zoe's brows drew together. "The
book I got said —"

"Book." He cursed automatically.
Keenan echoed him. "Sorry," he
muttered when Zoe gave him a
narrow-eyed look. "Now listen, you
learn how to add and subtract from
books. You don't learn baseball. Just
like a girl." He crouched down and
adjusted Keenan's hands.

Zoe had been ready to concede to
the expert, but the last statement
stopped her. "Excuse me? Are you
implying that females can't play
sports?"

"Not what I said. Swing from the

shoulders," he told Keenan. Coop might have been grouchy, but he wasn't stupid. "There are plenty of terrific female athletes. Keep your eye on the ball, kid." He kept one hand around Keenan's and lightly tossed the ball up in the air with the other. The bat connected with a hollow thud.

"I hit it! I hit it really, really hard!"

"Major league stuff." Coop slid his eyes back up to Zoe's. "I thought you were making pancakes."

"I was — I am." She blew out a breath. "I guess you're taking over."

"Well, I don't know diddly about pancakes, and you don't know squat about baseball. Why don't we both do what we know?"

"Like it's a big deal to hit a stupid ball with a stupid bat," she muttered as she strode to the back door.

"You can't do it."

She stopped dead in her tracks, eyes narrowed, turned. "I certainly can."

"Yeah, right. Okay, Keenan, let's try it again."

"I believe it's my turn." Challenge in her every movement, Zoe slipped the bat from her son's hands.

"Are you going to hit it, Mama? Are you?"

"You bet I am." She held out a hand for the ball Coop was holding. She tossed it up, swung, and batted the ball to the chain-link fence bordering the side yard. Keenan let out a cheer and raced to retrieve it.

Coop sniffed, smiled. "Not bad, for a girl. But anybody can hit a fungo."

"Keenan's too young for anything

114

but a plastic ball."

"No, a fungo's when you toss it up yourself and hit it."

"Oh."

"I'm gonna throw it, Coop. You catch."

"Sure, zip it in here."

It took Keenan three tries, running in closer each time, to send the ball anywhere near Coop.

"I suppose you don't think I could hit it if you threw it at me. . . ." Zoe began.

"Pitch it to you," Coop said patiently. "I would pitch it to you."

"All right, pitch it to me, then." She raised the bat.

"Fine, but you might want to turn a little more to the side. That's it," he said, backing away. "Zoe, you're holding the bat like you're going to use it to hammer a nail. Okay, here it comes."

He tossed the ball soft and underhand, but she still had to grit her teeth to keep herself from jerking away. Because her pride and her son's respect for women were at stake, she swung hard. No one was more stunned than Zoe when she connected. Coop snatched the ball an instant before it could smash his nose.

"Well." Zoe handed the bat back to a wide-eyed Keenan, dusted her hands. "I'll go see about those pancakes."

"She hit it really hard," Keenan said admiringly.

"Yeah." Coop watched the back door swing shut behind her. "Your mother's really . . . something, kid."

"Will you pitch to me, Coop? Will you?"

"Sure. But let's work on that stance, huh? You gotta look like a ballplayer."

When Zoe finished flipping the last pancake on the stack, she looked out the window and saw her son swing the bat. The ball didn't go far, but Coop made a pretense of a diving catch, missing, while Keenan danced gleefully in place.

"Too hot to handle," Coop claimed, and Keenan jumped on top of him. "Hey, there's no tackling in baseball. Football's out of season." He scooped the wriggling boy up and held him upside down. Somewhere along the line, his sour mood had vanished.

It became a habit to spend time

with the boy. Nothing planned, just playing a little catch in the yard or showing Keenan how to dunk baskets in the apartment. It wasn't as though he were attached to the kid, Coop assured himself. But when he had some free time and the boy wanted to hang around, what was the harm? Maybe it was sort of nice to see those big eyes all full of hero worship. And maybe it wasn't so much of a hardship to listen to that rollicking belly laugh Keenan burst into when something struck his fancy.

If the boy sometimes came along with the bonus of his mother, it wasn't exactly a hardship.

The fact was, he had seen a great deal more of Keenan than Zoe since the night of the thunderstorm. She was friendly enough, but she'd been careful — or so it seemed to Coop — not to be alone with him.

That was something he was going to fix, he decided as he shut down his computer.

He grabbed a couple of miniature race cars, some of the flotsam and jetsam of boyhood that Keenan had left in his apartment. If Coop knew Zoe as he thought he was beginning to, the toys would be an easier entry than a bouquet of long-stemmed roses.

Jiggling the cars in his hand, he strode down the steps to knock on her kitchen door.

In the laundry room, Zoe slammed down the lid on the washer. "Who is it?"

"It's Coop."

She hesitated, started the machine.

"Come on in. I'll be right out." She hefted a basket of clean laundry, as much out of defense as out of necessity, and went into the kitchen.

God, he looked good. She had really, really tried not to dwell on how good the man looked. So damn male, she thought, the rangy, athletic body, the muscles, the dark, untidy hair, and those wonderful pale green eyes. She wished her heart wouldn't always stutter when he aimed one of his cocky grins in her direction.

"Hi." She plopped the basket on the kitchen table and immediately began busying her hands folding socks.

"Hi." The kitchen was cluttered, as always. She really needed someone to help her organize, he thought. God, she smelled fantastic. "Keenan left these upstairs." Coop set the cars on the table. "I thought he might be looking for them."

"Thanks."

"So where is he?"

"In school."

"Oh, right." Coop knew Keenan's schedule as well as he knew yesterday's box scores. "You just get in from the flower shop?"

"Mmm-hmm . . . Business is picking up. We've got a couple of weddings. Actually, I could work full-time for the next three weeks, but it just doesn't fit Keenan's schedule."

"What do you mean?" Idly he plucked a shirt from the basket.

"Well, the spring weddings. The arrangements take a lot of extra hands, so Fred asked if I could put in full days for a while."

"So, that's good, right?"

"The school Keenan goes to is really more of a preschool than daycare. It doesn't stay open after three. And I have the car pool next week, anyway. Plus, I promised to take him and some of the other kids swimming at the community center on Friday. He's really looking forward to it."

"Yeah, he mentioned it." About twenty times, Coop recalled.

"I don't want to let him down."

"So, I'll do it."

She looked back up, socks dangling from her hands. "What?"

He couldn't believe he'd said that. He stared at her for another moment, then shrugged. "I said I'd do it. It's no big deal. He can hang with me when he gets home from school."

She tilted her head. "Don't you have a job?"

"That's what I call it, since they pay me." He smiled, finding the idea went down easily. "I do most of my writing here, and he could tag along when I go in to the paper or on an interview. He'd probably get a kick out of it."

"I'm sure he would." She narrowed her eyes. Why couldn't she get a handle on J. Cooper McKinnon? "But why would you?"

He wasn't sure he had the answer to that, so he punted. "Why not? He's not that much of a pest."

With a laugh, she went back to her laundry. "Maybe he's not, but you forgot the car pool."

"I can drive. What's the big deal about hauling a bunch of kids to

123

school and back?"

"I can't begin to tell you," she murmured. It was, perhaps, something every adult should experience for himself. "And the swimming."

"I was captain of the swim team in college. All-state."

She glanced up at that. "I thought you played baseball. Uh, Keenan mentioned it."

"Yeah, I did. Two hundred and twelve RBIs my last season. I played basketball, too, averaged forty-two points a game." He was bragging, Coop realized. Like some gawky teenager trying to impress the head cheerleader. He frowned down at the little cars, began to slide one over the table.

"Keenan says you make great engine noises."

"Yeah, it's a talent."

He'd embarrassed himself, Zoe realized, and she wanted to hug him. "Tell you what. Why don't we take it a day at a time? If you decide you can't handle it —"

His eyes flashed up at that. "I think I can handle one scrawny kid and a few of his pals."

"Okay. If you decide you don't *want* to handle it, no hard feelings."

"Fine. When do you want to start?"

"Tomorrow would be great."

"Okay." That was settled. Now, he thought, it was on to other business. "How about dinner?"

Her eyes widened in surprise. "Um . . . sure. We're just going to have chicken. I'll probably fry it."

"No." He stepped closer. She stepped back. "I mean, why don't we have dinner? Out. You and me."

"Oh, well . . ." Good answer, she thought foolishly. Very succinct. She took another step in retreat. "I have to work tonight."

"Tomorrow."

"I don't really go out."

"I've noticed. What are you backing away from, Zoe?"

"You." Annoyed with herself, she held up a hand. And found it pressed against his chest. "I don't want to date anyone. Start anything. I have very good reasons."

"You'll have to tell me about them sometime." He reached up, combed a hand through her hair and loosened the band that held it back.

"You're not going to kiss me again."

"Sure I am." He touched his lips to

hers to prove it. His eyes remained open as he drew her lower lip into his mouth, as he used his tongue, his teeth, to tease and seduce. "You've got an incredible mouth."

She couldn't get her breath. Even as she gasped for it, her vision dimmed. It was all she wanted. It seemed her life depended on keeping her lips against his. This wasn't fair, she thought dimly as she began to sink into the glory of sensation. Too long, she told herself. Surely she was reacting this way only because it had been so terribly long since she'd allowed herself to feel only as a woman.

She was melting against him like wax. He hadn't known how painfully erotic it would be to feel that long, lean body go fluid. He'd only meant to kiss her, to test them both, but his hands were already reaching, stroking, exploring.

His touch, those hard, callused hands against her bare skin, all but brought her to her knees.

"I have to think."

"Think later." He pressed his mouth to her throat.

Oh, it was glorious, glorious to ache again. But she knew too well what came from soothing that ache. "Coop, we can't do this."

"Yes, we can. I'll show you."

With a laugh that came out half moan, she turned her head away. "My head's spinning. You have to stop. God, do you have any idea what you're doing to me?"

"I haven't even started. Come upstairs, come upstairs with me, Zoe. I want to feel you under me. I want to feel myself inside you."

"I want to." She trembled, the needs exploding inside her like firebombs. "Coop, I need to think first. I have to think. I haven't been with anyone in five years."

His mouth stopped its desperate journey over her throat. Slowly he drew back to look at her. Her eyes were clouded, and her mouth was swollen and ripe. "No one?"

"No." She swallowed and prayed for her system to level before she gave in to the urge to rip off his clothes and cut loose. "Since before Keenan was born. I feel like all those needs dried up — like old leaves. You've set a match to them, and I don't know how to handle it."

"The kid's father," Coop said carefully. "You're still in love with him."

"No." She might have laughed at that, if she weren't so shaken. "He has nothing to do with it. Well, of course he does, but . . . I have to sit down." She walked unsteadily to a chair. "I knew this was going to happen. I think I knew it the first time I saw you. There's been no one, because I didn't want anyone. Because Keenan was all that mattered to me. I have plans." That came out as an accusation, and her eyes darkened. "Damn it, I have plans. I want to go back to school. I want to have my own flower shop one day." Her voice began to catch, alarming him.

"Zoe —"

But she barreled right over him. "And everything was going along fine. I got the house. I wanted him to have a house, and a yard, and neighbors. Everyone said I was crazy, that I'd never be able to do it, that I'd be sorry I'd given everything up to raise a child on my own. But I'm not sorry. He's the best thing that ever happened to me. And I've done a good job. Keenan's happy, and he's bright and funny and wonderful. We have a good life, and I know I can make it even better. I haven't needed anyone. And . . . Oh, God, I'm in love with you."

The hand he'd lifted awkwardly to pat her head froze. "What?"

"Oh, what a mess. What a mess." She plucked a tiny sock out of the laundry basket and wiped her eyes. "Maybe it's just hormones. It could be, you know. But I walked in and you were sleeping with him on the couch. It was so sweet. Then you were kissing me and everything went crazy. Then you're out in the yard looking so smug and male, showing Keenan how to hit that silly ball. And you're eating pancakes and looking at me. I can hardly breathe when you're looking at me."

Somewhere along the line, his mind had gone blank. "I think I missed a step."

"No, you didn't." She sniffled and struggled to get herself under control. "I've just taken too many. It's my fault. You've been nice to Keenan, and you've been honest with me." She sighed, dropped the damp sock in her lap. "Believe me, I know my emotions are my responsibility." Because he was still staring at her, like a man who'd just had the friendly family dog lunge for his throat, she smiled. "I'm sorry, Coop. I shouldn't have dumped all that on you. I didn't even know it was all bottled up."

This time he took a step back. "Zoe, I like the kid. Who wouldn't? And I'm attracted to you. But —"

"There's no need to explain." Steady now, she rose. "Really, there isn't. I don't expect anything from you, and I'm sorry if I made you uncomfortable. But I feel a lot better." And, oddly enough, she did. "When I go to bed with you, we'll understand each other."

"When you —"

"I think we both know that's going to happen," she said calmly. "We both want it to, and it's smarter to face that than to live with all this tension. Keenan's been wanting to spend the night with a friend of his.

I'll arrange it." She laughed a little at Coop's expression. "It's a little hard to be spontaneous with a four-year-old around. I hope you don't mind planning out a night together."

"No, I mean, I don't — God, Zoe."

"If you'd rather not, or if you want some time to decide, that's all right."

He studied her face, felt that same greedy tug, and a flare of something entirely different. Entirely new. "No, I want you. Whenever."

"How about Monday night?"

"I've got a twilight doubleheader on Monday." He couldn't believe he was standing here planning out a wild night of love like a dentist's appointment.

"Ah . . . Wednesday?"

He nodded. "Wednesday's good

for me. Do you want to go out somewhere?"

It was sweet, she thought, really
sweet of him to ask. "It's not neces-
sary." She laid a hand on his cheek. "I
don't need flowers and candlelight.
I'll come upstairs after Keenan's settled."

"Good. Fine. I . . . better get back
to work."

"Do you still want to have Keenan
tomorrow?"

"Yeah, no problem. Tell him to
come on up." Coop backed toward
the door as Zoe began folding
laundry again. "I guess I'll see you."

She listened to him walk up the
steps. He was certainly a mistake, she
told herself. But she'd made others.
Life got too mundane when you
avoided all the wrong turns.

Chapter 7

"He shoots, he scores!" Coop made appropriate crowd noises as Keenan dunked the basket.

"I can do it again! I can, okay?" From his perch on Coop's shoulders, Keenan swung his sneakered feet.

"Okay, you've drawn the foul." Coop scooped the palm-sized ball up and passed it into Keenan's eager hands. "It's game point, kid, ten seconds to play. This free throw is all-or-nothing. Got it?"

"Got it!"

"A hush falls over the crowd as Fleming steps up to the line. He's played the game of his life tonight, but it all comes down to this one shot.

He eyes the basket. You eyeing the basket?"

"Eyeing it," Keenan said, with his tongue caught between his teeth.

"He sets . . . and shoots." Coop winced as the little rubber ball circled the rim, then watched through squinted eyes as it tipped in and dropped through the net.

"And the crowd goes wild!" Coop danced around the sofa while Keenan hooted and clapped on his shoulders. When he dumped the boy on the cushions of the sofa, Keenan let go with one of the rolling belly laughs that always made Coop grin. "You're a natural."

"You shoot it, Coop! You!"

Obliging, Coop executed a quick turnaround jump shot. This wasn't such a bad way to spend a rainy afternoon, he decided. And it helped keep his mind off how he was going to spend the rainy night ahead.

It was Wednesday.

"Okay, time out. I've got to finish up my piece on the track meet."

"Are we going to go to the paper again? It's neat there."

"Not today. I'm going to fax it in when it's done. You watch some tube." Coop hit the remote, then handed it over.

"Can I get a drink?"

"Yeah, there's some of that juice your mom sent up for you. Stay out of trouble, right?"

"Right."

When Coop headed into his office, Keenan scrambled up from the couch. He liked it best when he got to stay with Coop after school. They always got to do something neat, and Coop never asked if he'd washed his hands or said too many cookies would spoil his appetite.

Best of all, he liked when Coop picked him up. It was different than when his mother did. He liked when she held him, nuzzled him after his bath or rocked him when he had a bad dream. But Coop smelled different, and felt different.

He knew why, Keenan thought as he wandered into the kitchen. It was because Coop was a daddy instead of a mom.

He liked to pretend Coop was his daddy, and figured that maybe if he didn't do anything bad, Coop wouldn't go away.

After a couple of tugs, Keenan had the refrigerator open. He was proud that Coop had hung the pictures he had drawn for him on the door. He peered inside, saw the jug of juice his mother had bought for him. And the green bottles Coop liked.

"B-E-E-R," Keenan said to himself. He remembered that he'd asked Coop if he could have a taste from the bottle, and that Coop had told him he couldn't until he was big. After Coop had let him sniff the beer, Keenan had been glad he wasn't big yet.

There was a new bottle in the fridge today, and Keenan knit his brow and tried to recognize the letters. *C-H-A-R-D-O-N* — There were too many letters to read, so he lost interest.

He took out the jug, gripping it manfully and setting it on the floor. Humming to himself, he dragged a chair over to get cups from the cabinet. One day he'd be as tall as Coop and wouldn't need to stand on a chair. He leaned forward on his toes.

The crash and the howl had Coop leaping up, rapping his knee hard against the desk. Papers scattered as he raced out of the office and into the kitchen.

Keenan was still howling. A chair was overturned, juice was glugging cheerfully onto the floor, and the refrigerator was wide open. Coop splashed through the puddle and scooped Keenan up.

"Are you hurt? What'd you do?" When his only answer was another sob, he stood Keenan on the kitchen table and searched for blood. He imagined gaping wounds, broken bones.

"I fell down." Keenan wriggled

back into Coop's arms.

"Okay, it's okay. Did you hit your head?"

"Nuh-uh." With a sniffle, Keenan waited for the kisses he expected after a hurt. "I fell on my bottom." Keenan's lip poked out. "Kiss it."

"You want me to kiss your — Come on, kid, you're joking."

The lip trembled, another tear fell. "You gotta kiss where it hurts. You gotta, or it won't get better."

"Oh, man." Flummoxed, Coop dragged a hand through his hair. He was desperately relieved that no blood had been spilled, but if anyone, anyone, found out what he was about to do, he'd never live it down. He turned Keenan around and gave the little rump a quick kiss. "Does that do it?"

"Uh-huh." Keenan knuckled his eyes, then held out his arms. "Will you pick me up?"

"Yeah." He didn't feel as ridiculous as he'd expected when the boy's arms went around his neck. "Okay now?"

With his head resting on Coop's shoulder, he nodded. "I didn't mean to do it. I spilled all the juice."

"No big deal." Hardly realizing he did so, Coop turned his head to brush his lips over Keenan's hair. Something was shifting inside him, creaking open.

"You aren't mad at me? You won't go away?"

"No." What the hell was going on? Coop wondered as unexplored and unexpected emotions swirled inside him. "No, I'm not going anywhere."

"I love you," Keenan said, with the

simple ease of a child.

Coop closed his eyes and wondered how a grown man was supposed to handle falling for a four-year-old boy.

Well, here she was, Zoe thought as she stood at the bottom of the steps leading to Coop's apartment. All she had to do was go upstairs, open the door and start an affair. Her stomach clenched.

Silly to be nervous, she told herself, and climbed the first step. She was a normal woman with normal needs. If her emotions were too close to the surface, she would deal with it. It was much more difficult to be hurt when you had no expectations.

She'd had expectations once, but she knew better now.

This was simply a physical attraction between two single, healthy people. She'd nearly backed down a step before she forced herself to move forward. All the practical details had been seen to. Her son was safely tucked away for the night at his sleepover. She'd arranged for birth control — that wasn't an oversight she would make again.

No regrets, she promised herself as she lifted a hand to knock. She knew how useless they were.

He answered so quickly, she nearly jumped. Then they stood and stared at each other.

She'd worn a dress, one of those thin, breezy sundresses designed to make a man give thanks for the end of winter. Her hair was loose, falling over thin raspberry-colored straps and bare, peach-toned shoulders.

There were nerves in her eyes.

"Hi." He glanced down to the cordless phone she held. "Expecting a call?"

"What? Oh." She laughed, miserably self-conscious. "No, I just don't like to be out of touch when Keenan's not home."

"He's all settled at his pal's?"

"Yeah." She stepped inside, set the phone on the counter. "He was so excited, he —" She broke off when her sandal stuck to the floor.

Coop grimaced. "I guess I missed some of it. We had a spill."

"Oh?"

"The kid took a tumble, sheared off ten years of my life. No blood lost, though. Just a half gallon of orange juice." When she only smiled, he stepped to the refrigerator. Why in

146

hell was he babbling? "Want some wine?"

"That would be nice." Why, he's as nervous as I am, she realized, and she loved him for it. "Keenan's having a wonderful time staying with you. I have to study the sports pages now just to keep up with what he's talking about."

"He catches on fast."

"So do I. Go ahead," she said as he handed her a glass of wine, "Ask me about stats. I know all about RBIs and ERAs." She took a sip, then gestured with her glass. "I think the Orioles would have taken the second game of that doubleheader the other night if they'd put in a relief pitcher in the second inning."

His lips twitched. "Do you?"

"Well, the starter had lost his stuff,

obviously. The guy who was announcing —"

"The play-by-play man."

"Yes, he said so himself."

"So, you watched the game."

"I watch 'Sesame Street,' too. I like to keep up with Keenan's interests." She trailed off when Coop reached out to twine a lock of her hair around his finger.

"He's got a thing for dinosaurs, too."

"I know, I've checked a half dozen books out of the library. We've —" The fingers trailed over her shoulder. "We've been down to the natural history museum twice."

She set the glass aside and fell into his arms.

He kissed her as though he'd been starved for her taste. The impact was fast, deep, desperate. The little purring sounds that vibrated in her throat had his muscles turning into bundles of taut wire.

"I wasn't sure you'd come."

"Neither was I. I —"

"Can't think of anything but you," he said as he swept her off her feet. "I thought we'd take this slow."

"Let's not," she murmured, pressing her lips to his throat as he carried her into the bedroom.

She had a quick impression of Spartan neatness and simple masculine colors and lines before they tumbled onto the bed.

Neither of them was looking for patience. They rolled together, a tangle of limbs grasping, groping, glorying. The sheer physicality of it, flesh to flesh, mouth to mouth, had Zoe's head reeling. Oh, she wanted to be touched like this, to feel so desperately like a woman, with a man's hand streaking over her, with his lips savoring every thud of her pulse.

So she lost herself. No more nerves, no more fears. And if she loved, it only made the joy of mating more lovely.

She was every man's fantasy. Stunningly responsive, breathlessly aggressive. And so beautiful, he thought. Undraped, the exquisite body was so slim, so perfect, he couldn't believe it had ever carried a child. In the gilded light of dusk, her face was elegant, heart-stopping. Whenever he touched, wherever he touched, he could see the bold echo of her pleasure reflected in her eyes.

He watched those eyes glaze over,

felt her body tense, heard her stran-
gled cry of release. Swamped with
the power of it, he drove her upward
again until they were both panting
for air, until she reared up from the
bed and wrapped herself around
him.

Damp skin slid over damp skin,
hungry mouth sought hungry mouth.
They rolled over the bed again,
moaning, quivering. Then his hands
gripped hers, and his mouth crushed
her mouth. And he thrust inside her,
hard and deep.

She felt the sensation as if it were a
lance through her system, painful,
glorious. For an instant, neither of
them moved, they just stayed tensed
and shuddering on the edge.

Then it was all movement, all
speed, a wild race that ended with

them both plunging deliriously over the finish line.

It wasn't exactly the way he'd imagined, Coop thought. They were sprawled across his bed, Zoe curled against him. The light was nearly gone, and the room was full of shadows.

He'd imagined they would progress to the bedroom by stages. They were both adults and had known that was the ultimate goal, but he'd thought they would move slowly.

Then she'd been standing there smiling, the nerves shining in her eyes . . . He'd never wanted anything or anyone more in his life.

Still, he thought she deserved more than a quick tussle, however rewarding. But the night was young.

He flexed his arm to bring her head a little closer, brushed his lips over her temple. "Okay?"

"Mmm . . . At the very least." Her body felt golden. She was surprised her skin didn't glow in the dark.

"I rushed you a little."

"No, perfect timing."

He began to trail a finger up and down her arm. He wanted her again. Good God, his system was already churning to life. A little control, Coop, he ordered himself. "You're going to stay?"

She opened her eyes, looking into his. "Yes."

"I'm going to go get the wine."

"That's good." She sighed as he left the bed. She'd forgotten how to deal with the after, she realized. Or with the before and during, for that matter, she thought with a wry smile. Though she thought she'd done pretty well so far.

She hadn't known how much had been bottled up inside her. Or just how much she'd needed to feel like a woman again. But then, she hadn't known she could love again.

She shifted, slipping under the tangled sheets, automatically lifting them to her breasts when Coop came back with the wine and glasses.

The sight of her in his bed shot to his loins, with a quick detour through the heart. He said nothing, pouring wine, offering her a fresh glass and settling beside her.

"Why haven't you been with anyone?" The moment the question was out, he wished for a rusty knife to hack off his tongue. "Sorry, none of my business."

"It's all right." Because I haven't fallen in love with anyone before you, she thought. But that wasn't what he wanted to hear, she knew. Nor was it really what he'd asked.

"You want to know about Keenan's father."

"None of my business," he repeated. "Sorry, it's the reporter in me."

"It was a long time ago — a lifetime ago. I don't mind telling you. I grew up in New York. I think I mentioned that my mother's an actress. I was the result of a second marriage. She's had five. So far."

"Five?"

Zoe chuckled into her wine, sipped. "Clarice falls in love and changes husbands the way some women change hairstyles. My father lasted about four years before they parted amicably. Clarice always has friendly divorces. I didn't see much of him, because he moved to Hollywood. He does commercials and voice-overs mostly. Anyway, I think she was on husband number four when I was in high school. He had some pull with the Towers Modeling Agency. They're pretty big."

"I've heard of them."

"Well, he got me in. I started doing some shoots. And I caught on."

"That's it," Coop said, interrupting her. "I knew I'd seen your face before."

She moved her shoulders. "Five, six years ago, it was hard to avoid it. I did twenty covers in one month, the year after I graduated school."

"Cover of *In Sports*, swimsuit edition."

She smiled. "You've got a good memory. That was six years ago."

He remembered the long, sand-dusted legs, the lush wet red excuse for a bathing suit, the laughing, seductive face. He gulped down wine. "It was a hell of a shot."

"And a long, grueling shoot. Anyway, I was making a lot of money, getting a lot of press, going to lots of parties. I met Roberto at one of them."

"Roberto." Coop grimaced at the sound of the name.

"Lorenzi. Tennis player. You might have heard of him."

"Lorenzi? Sure — took the French Open three years ago in straight sets, then blew Wimbledon in the semis.

He's got a bad attitude and likes to race cars and chase women on the side. Hasn't been seeded above twenty-fifth in the last two years. Got some bad press this spring when he tipped back too many vinos and punched out a photographer." Coop started to drink, stopped. "Lorenzi? He's Keenan's father? But he's —"

"A womanizer?" Zoe supplied. "A creep, a rich, spoiled egotist? I know — now. What I saw then was a gorgeous, charming man who sent me roses and jetted me off to Monte Carlo for intimate dinners. I was dazzled. He told me he loved me, that he adored me, worshiped me, he couldn't live without me. I believed him, and we became lovers. I thought, since he was my first, he'd be my only. Anyway, I didn't realize he was already getting tired of me when I found out I was pregnant. When I told him, he was angry, then he was very calm, very reasonable. He assumed I'd want an abortion and agreed to pay all the expenses, even to make the arrangements."

"A real prince."

"It was a logical assumption," Zoe said calmly. "I had a career on fast forward, in a field that wouldn't wait while I put on weight and suffered from morning sickness. He, of course, had no intention of marrying me, and thought, rightly enough, that I knew the rules of the game. I did know them," she said quietly. "But something had changed when the doctor confirmed the pregnancy. After the disbelief, the panic, even the anger, I felt good. I felt right. I wanted the baby, so I quit my job, moved away from New York and read everything I could get my hands on about parenting."

"Just like that?"

"Well, there were some scenes, some dire predictions, and a lot of anger, but that's how it worked. Roberto and I parted less than amicably, but with the agreement that he would stay out of my life and I would stay out of his."

"What have you told Keenan?"

"It's tough." And it never failed to make her feel guilty. "So far I've just told him his father had to go away, that he wasn't going to come back. He's happy, so he doesn't ask a lot of questions."

"Are you? Happy?"

"Yes." She smiled and touched his

cheek. "I am. All my life I wanted a home, a family, something solid and settled. I didn't even know it until Keenan. He changed my life."

"No urge to go back and smile for the camera?"

"Oh, no. Not even a twinge."

He cupped a hand behind her neck, studying her. "It's such a face," he murmured. Right now he liked the idea of having it all to himself.

Chapter 8

The concept of car pools obviously had been devised by someone with a foul and vicious sense of humor. Having lived most of his life in cities where public transportation or a quick jog would get a man from his home to his office, Coop had never experienced the adult version.

But he'd heard rumors.

Arguments, petty feuds, crowded conditions, spilled coffee.

After a week as designated driver, Coop had no doubt the kiddie version was worse. Infinitely worse.

"He's pinching me again, Mr. McKinnon. Brad's pinching me."

"Cut it out, Brad."

"Carly's looking at me. I told her to stop looking at me."

"Carly, don't look at Brad."

"I'm going to be sick. Mr. McKinnon, I'm going to be sick right now."

"No, you're not."

Though Matthew Finney made gagging noises that had the other kids screeching, Coop gritted his teeth and kept driving. Matt threatened to be sick twice a day unless he rode in the front seat. After five miserable days Coop had his number. But that did very little to soothe his nerves.

Keenan, who had waited all week for his turn in the front, swiveled in his seat to make monster faces at Matt. This incited a small riot of elbow jabs, howls, screaming giggles and shoves.

"Keenan, turn around!" Coop snapped. "You guys straighten up back there. Cut it out! If I have to stop this car . . ." He trailed off, shuddered. He'd sounded like his own mother. Now Coop was afraid *he* would be sick. "Okay, first stop. Matt, scram."

Fifteen minutes later, his back seat thankfully empty, Coop pulled into the drive and rested his throbbing head on the steering wheel. "I need a drink."

"We got lemonade," Keenan told him.

"Great." He reached over to unbuckle Keenan's seat belt. All he needed was a pint of vodka to go with it.

"Can we go swimming again soon?"

The idea of taking a herd of screaming kids back to the community pool anytime within the next century had a stone lodging in Coop's heart. "Ask your mother."

Coop started to look in the back seat and realized he couldn't face it. Earlier in the week he'd made that mistake, and discovered wads of chewing gum on the rug, cookie crumbs everywhere, and a mysterious green substance smeared on the seat.

In his weakened state, even a candy wrapper was likely to tip the balance.

"Yoo-hoo!" Mrs. Finkleman stripped off her flowered garden gloves and headed across the lawn in a flowing tent dress and electric-blue sandals. "How was your swim, little man?"

"We had races, and Brad dunked

Carly and made her cry even though Coop told him not to, and I can hold my breath underwater for twelve seconds."

"My goodness." She laughed and ruffled Keenan's hair. "You'll be in the Olympics next." Her shrewd eyes took in Coop's haggard face. "You look a little frazzled, Coop. Keenan, why don't you run in and tell Mr. Finkleman you want a piece of that cherry cobbler he baked today?"

"Okay!" He tugged on Coop's hand. "Do you want some? Do you wanna come?"

"I'll pass. You go ahead."

Mrs. Finkleman chuckled as Keenan darted away and scrambled up the steps. "Little angel. We'll keep him entertained for a couple of hours — or he'll keep us entertained. You look like you could use a few minutes in a quiet room."

"Padded room," Coop muttered. "How does anyone survive kids?"

"It's easier if you go through the stages with them. Once you've walked the floor all night with a col-icky baby, nothing much fazes you." She sighed. "Except science projects. Science projects always took me to the edge. And that first driving lesson." She shook her head at the memory. "That can bring you to your knees." She beamed and patted his arm. "But there's years yet to worry about that. And you've been doing a fine job. Why, Harry and I were just saying how nice it is that Zoe and Keenan have a man in their lives. Not that Zoe hasn't been handling every-thing. Raising that sweet-natured boy all alone, and working two jobs and tending the house. But it does my heart good to see you and that little angel playing ball in the yard, or the way Zoe lights up when you're around. You make a lovely little family. Now, you go and take a nice nap. We'll keep an eye on your boy."

"I'm not — He's not —" But even as Coop stammered, she was drifting away.

Family? he thought as a ball of ice formed in his stomach. They weren't a family. Oh, no, he promised himself as he walked around the house to his steps. He hadn't taken that on.

He liked the kid, sure. What wasn't to like? And he was damn near nuts about the mother. But that didn't make them a family. That didn't make things permanent. Maybe he'd volunteered to spend time with the kid, taught him a few things about ball, pitched him a few, but that didn't make him Daddy.

He headed straight for the refrigerator, popped the top off a beer and took a long pull.

Sure, maybe he enjoyed having the kid around, and Lord knows he enjoyed being with Zoe. He'd even been sort of pleased when a woman at the pool mistook Keenan for his and commented on what a handsome son he had. But that didn't mean he was going to start thinking about family health insurance or college funds.

He was single. He liked being single. It meant coming and going as he pleased, planning all-night poker games, spending all day with the sports channel blaring.

He liked working in his own space — that was why he did the bulk of his writing at home, rather than at the paper. He didn't like people messing with his things or structuring his time or planning outings.

Family life — as he remembered from his childhood — was lousy with outings.

No way was he changing his nice comfortable existence to accommodate a family.

So he'd made a mistake, Coop decided, and stretched out on the couch with his beer. He'd given Zoe and the kid a little too much of his time, a little too much of his attention. It hadn't been anything he didn't want to give, but he could see now that the gesture could be misconstrued. Particularly since Zoe had once brought up the *L* word. Only once, he reminded himself, and he'd like to think that had just been a woman thing.

Still, if he didn't back off, they might start to depend on him. He shifted uncomfortably as the idea flitted through his mind that he might also come to depend on them.

It was time to reestablish himself as the tenant upstairs.

Keenan raced out of the house next door the minute his mother pulled her car in the drive.

"Hi, Mama, hi! I held my breath for twelve seconds underwater!"

Zoe caught him on the fly and swung him twice. "You must be hiding gills in there," she said, tickling his ribs. "Hi, Mrs. Finkleman."

"Hi yourself. We've had ourselves a fine hour. I sent Coop up for a nap when they got home. He looked like he'd had a rough day."

"Thanks." She kissed Keenan's waiting lips, then smacked her own. "Mmm . . . Cherries."

"Mr. Finkleman baked them, and they were good."

"I bet. Did you say thank you?"

"Uh-huh. Matt almost throwed up in Coop's car."

"Threw up," Zoe said as she carried Keenan inside.

"Uh-huh. 'Cause it was my turn to ride in the front. I had the best time, and Coop helped me to swim without my bubbles. He said I was a champ."

"That's just what you are." She collapsed with him on a chair. The idea of fixing dinner, changing into her uniform and serving drinks for six hours loomed heavily. "Give me a hug," she demanded, then soothed herself with some nuzzling. "Definitely a champion hugger. Why don't you come in the kitchen and tell me what else you did today while I fix dinner?"

A half hour later, as Zoe was draining pasta and Keenan was entertaining himself with crayons and paper on the kitchen floor, she heard the sound of Coop's feet on the stairs. Her heart sped up. The normal, healthy reaction made her smile. Imagine, she thought, believing herself immune to men.

She left the pasta draining in the sink and went to the back door just as he came to the foot of the steps.

"Hi."

"How's it going?" Coop jingled the keys in his pocket. Did she look all lit up? he wondered. She was smiling, and despite the shadows of fatigue under them, her eyes did have the prettiest lights in them.

"I was just going to call upstairs. I thought you'd like some dinner after a hard day at the pool." She opened the screen door and leaned out to kiss him. The smile dimmed a bit when he eased back. "It's just chicken and pasta."

It smelled nearly as good as she did. He glanced inside — the homey scene, cluttered counters, fresh flowers, steam rising from a pan on the stove, the child sprawled on the floor, the pretty woman offering him food and kisses.

A definite trap.

"Thanks, but I'm on my way out."

"Oh. I thought you had a couple hours before game time." She laughed at his arched brow. "I guess I've been paying more attention to the sports scene. Baltimore versus Toronto, game one of three."

"Yeah." When she starts to take an interest in *your* interests, she's really shutting the cage door. "I've got some stuff to do."

"Can I go with you?" Keenan dashed to the door to tug on Coop's slacks. "Can I go to the game? I like watching them with you best."

Coop could almost hear the locks clicking into place. "I've got too much to do," he said, with an edge to his voice that had Keenan's lips quivering. "Look, it's not just a game, it's my job."

"You said I was good luck."

"Keenan." Zoe put her hand on her son's shoulder to draw him back, but her eyes stayed on Coop's. "Did you forget Beth was coming over to stay with you tonight? She'll be here soon, and you're going to watch a tape of your favorite movie."

"But I wanna —"

"Now go wash your hands for dinner."

"But —"

"Go on now."

The way Keenan's face crumpled would have softened an ogre's heart. Dragging his feet, he headed out of the kitchen.

"I can't take him with me everywhere. . . ." Coop began defensively.

"Of course not. He's just overtired. I couldn't have let him go, in any case." She hesitated, wishing she could ignore her instincts. "Is everything all right?"

"Everything's fine." He didn't know why he shouted it. He didn't know why he felt like something slimy stuck to the bottom of a shoe. "I have a life, you know. I don't need kids climbing up my back or you fixing me dinner. And I don't have to explain myself."

Her eyes turned very cool, her face very composed. "You certainly don't. I appreciate you helping me out the past couple of weeks. Let me know if I can return the favor."

"Look, Zoe —"

"I've got to get dinner on the table, or I'll be late for work." She let the screen door slam between them. "Enjoy the game."

She knew exactly how long he continued to stand there while she worked at the stove. Knew exactly when he turned and walked away.

It wasn't unexpected, she reminded herself. This backing away was typical, even understandable. Perhaps it had taken Coop a few weeks to completely comprehend that she didn't come as a single. She was part of a pair, a ready-made family, with its share of responsibilities and problems and routines.

And he was opting out.

He might not even know it yet, she thought, but he was in the first stages of a full retreat.

Her eyes blurred, her chest heaved. Resolutely she choked the tears back. She would indulge herself with a nice long cry later, she promised. But for now she had a little boy to soothe.

When he came back in, she crouched down until they were eye-to-eye.

"You had a good time with Coop today, didn't you?"

Keenan sniffled, nodded.

"And he's taken you a lot of places. You've had fun, and done a lot of new things."

"I know."

"You should be grateful for that, baby, instead of pouting because you can't have more."

She straightened again and hoped she could take her own advice.

Chapter 9

"You're spending a lot of time around here." Ben edged a hip onto the corner of Coop's desk. All around Coop's cubicle phones rang, keyboards clattered.

"So?" Without taking his eyes from the computer screen, Coop hammered out the draft of his weekly column.

"I just figured you had it made in that apartment of yours. I mean, great location." He thought of Zoe. "Great view. You didn't spend as much time in here when you lived downtown."

"I needed a change of scene."

"Yeah." Ben snorted and picked up

a baseball from Coop's desk. "Trouble in paradise?"

"I don't know what you're talking about. And I've got a column to write."

"Pretty obvious the last few weeks that you've been stuck on the landlady." He tossed the ball from one hand to the other. "I mean, when a man hauls a kid around, buys little baseball jerseys, it follows that he's hooking a line into Mom."

Coop's eyes flashed up. "I like the kid, okay? I don't have to use a four-year-old to get a woman. The kid's cool."

"Hey, I got nothing against rug rats. Might even have a few of my own one day. The thing is, when a woman's got one, a man has to play Daddy if he wants the inside track."

"Who says I have to play at anything to get a woman?"

"Not me. But it was you who couldn't shoot hoop last week because you were taking the family to the aquarium." Ben winked, set the ball down. "Still, I bet you scored better than I did." Ben jerked back as Coop lunged for his throat.

"It's not like that," Coop said between his teeth.

"Hey, hey. Just yanking your chain. I wouldn't have made any cracks if I'd known you were serious about her."

Coop's grip loosened. "I didn't say I was serious. I said it wasn't like that."

"Whatever you say."

Disgusted with himself, Coop dropped back in his chair. He and

Ben had been riding each other about women for better than five years. No reason to overreact, he thought. Or to make a fool of himself. "Sorry. I've got a lot on my mind."

"Forget it. What you need's a distraction. You coming to the poker game tonight?"

"Yeah."

"Good. Losing money should put you back on track."

Something had to, Coop thought as he sat back alone in his cubicle to stare at his screen. For the past three days he'd slept little, eaten less, and gone around in a constant state of flux.

Because he was avoiding the issue, he decided. Opting to bunt, when he should be swinging away. The only solution to getting his life back in order was to face the problem head-on.

He flicked off his terminal.

The beautiful thing about an afternoon off, Zoe thought, was the solitude. No customers to talk to, no orders to fill. It meant she didn't have to be salesclerk, or waitress, or Mom, or anything but Zoe.

Sitting on the back stoop, she struggled to understand the assembly instructions for the new barbecue grill she'd bought. She was going to surprise Keenan with hamburgers.

She liked the quiet — her kind of quiet, which meant there was music throbbing from the kitchen radio. She liked the loneliness — her kind of loneliness, which meant Keenan would dash toward her shortly with open arms and chattering voice.

She knew the upstairs apartment was empty, and she tried not to think about that. Tried not to think about the fact that Coop had been away more than he'd been home in the last few days.

Foolish of her to have thought he was different. He'd wanted her, he'd had her, and now he'd lost interest. Well, she had wanted him, so they were even there. If her heart was suffering it would pass. It had passed before. She and Keenan could get along fine on their own. Just like always.

Her screwdriver slipped, scraped her knuckles, had her swearing.

"What the hell are you doing?"

Eyes hot, she looked up at Coop. "Baking a cake. What does it look like I'm doing?"

"You can't put something together if you're going to spread parts all over the damn place." Automatically he bent down to organize. She rapped his hand away with the rubber grip of the screwdriver.

"I don't need you to put things together for me. I'm not some poor helpless female who needs a man to pick up the slack. I managed just fine before you came along."

Stung, he rammed his hands in his pockets. "Fine. Do it yourself."

"I am doing it myself. I like doing it myself."

"Terrific. And when the thing topples over, you won't have anyone else to blame."

"That's right." She blew her hair out of her eyes. "I accept when something's my fault." She picked up a wrench and locked a bolt in place. "Do you plan to hover over me all afternoon?"

"I want to talk to you."

"So talk."

He had it well planned. He was a writer, after all. "I realize the way I've been hanging around with you and the kid —"

"His name is Keenan," Zoe said between her teeth.

"I know what his name is. The way I've been hanging around the last few weeks might give the wrong impression."

"Oh, really?" She looked up again, tapping the wrench against her palm.

"He's a great kid, he kind of grows on you. I've gotten a kick out of spending time with him."

Though she hated herself for it, Zoe

softened. She understood that he was genuinely fond of Keenan. That only made it all the more difficult. "He likes spending time with you. It's been good for him."

"Well, yeah, on the one hand. On the other, I started thinking that he — that you — that both of you might get the wrong idea. I mean, tossing a ball around or taking him to a game, that's cool. I just don't want him thinking it's like — permanent."

"I see." She was calm now, frigidly so. It would help keep the hurt in check. "You're afraid he might begin to see you as a father figure."

"Well, yeah. Kind of."

"That's natural enough. But then, he spends a lot of time with Mr. Finkleman, too, and with Billy Bowers down the street."

"Finkleman's old enough to be his grandfather, and the Bowers kid is eighteen." Coop backed off, realizing there was a touch of jealousy in the defense. "And they don't have the same sort of thing going with you."

She arched both brows. "Thing?"

"Relationship," he said tightly. "Whatever the hell you want to call it. Damn it, we only slept together once."

"I'm aware of that." Carefully she set the wrench aside. It would give her only momentary pleasure to heave it at his head.

"That came out wrong," he said, furious with himself. "It sounded like it didn't mean anything. It did, Zoe." A great deal, he was afraid. A very great deal. "It's just that . . ."

"Now you're terrified that Keenan

and I will trap you into a family. That you'll wake up one morning and be Daddy, with a wife and a mortgage and a small boy who needs attention."

"Yes. No. Something like that." He was burying himself, he realized, and he suddenly didn't know why. "I just want to make myself clear."

"Oh, I think you have. Perfectly." She rubbed her hands on her knees as she studied him. "You needn't worry, Coop. I advertised for a tenant, not a father for my child, or a husband for myself. I slept with you because I wanted to, not because I thought I could lure you to the altar."

"I didn't mean it like that." Frustrated, he dragged a hand through his hair. However well he'd planned this little scene, it was going all wrong. "I wanted you. I still do. But I know how badly you were let down before. I don't want to hurt you, Zoe. Or the kid. I just don't want you thinking I'd slide into the gap."

The anger came back, one swift wave of it that reddened her vision. She was on her feet before either of them realized she'd moved. "Keenan and I don't have a gap. We're a family, as real and as complete and as full a family as any could be." She jabbed the wrench at his chest. "Just because Daddy doesn't make three doesn't mean we're less of a unit."

"I didn't mean —"

"I'll tell you what you mean. You see a woman and a small boy and you think they're just pining away for some big strong man to come along and fulfill them. Well, that's bull. If I needed a man, I'd have one. And if I thought Keenan needed a father to make him happy, I'd find him one. And," she continued, advancing and giving him another jab, "if you think you're at the head of some fictional list, you're wrong. Maybe I'm in love with you, but that's not enough. It's not just me, and it's not just you. Keenan comes first. When and if I want a father for Keenan, he'll be someone with compassion and patience, someone willing to adjust his life to make room for my son. So relax, Cooper. You're in the clear."

"I didn't come here to fight with you."

"Good, because I'm finished."

He grabbed her arm before she could turn away. "I haven't. I'm trying to be straight with you, Zoe. I care about you, okay? About both of you. I just don't want it to get out of hand."

"Out of whose hands?" she retorted. "Yours? Then that's no problem, is it? Because you know how to hold on to everything inside, really tight. Just keep holding on to it, Coop. Don't worry about me or about Keenan. We'll be fine." She jerked her arm free and sat again. Picking up the instruction sheet, she gave it her full attention.

Now why, he wondered, did he feel as though he'd just been rejected? Shaking his head, Coop took a step in retreat. "As long as we're clear."

"We are."

"I've, ah, got a little time, if you want me to help you put that grill together."

"No thanks. I can do it." She slanted him a look. "I'm going to grill burgers later. You're welcome to join us. Unless you're afraid it will lead to a commitment."

She shoots, he thought wryly, she scores. "Thanks anyway. I've got plans. Maybe I could take a rain check."

"Fine. You know where to find us."

He got drunk. Not sloppily, but thoroughly. When Coop poured himself out of the cab and staggered toward the house, he already knew he'd hate himself in the morning. But it was tonight he had to deal with.

He leaned heavily against Zoe's front door and waited for the porch to settle down under his feet. She might think they'd finished, he told himself blearily, but she was wrong. Dead wrong.

He'd thought of a dozen things he had to say to her.

There was no time like the present.

Lifting a fist, he pounded on the door. "Come on, Zoe." He pounded again. "I know you're in there." He saw a light flick on inside and kept on pounding. "Come on, come on. Open up."

"Coop?" From the other side of the door, Zoe belted her hastily donned robe. She'd been home from the lounge for barely twenty minutes, and in bed for less than five. "It's after two o'clock in the morning. What do you want?"

"I want to talk to you. Let me in."

"We'll talk in the morning."

"You just said it was morning."

195

When he pounded again, she flicked off the locks. "Stop that — you'll wake Keenan." Furious, she yanked open the door and had the surprise of a hundred-and-seventy-pound male tumbling against her. "Are you hurt? What happened?" The alarm signals that had screamed on shifted when she caught the scent of beer. "You're drunk."

"Mostly." He started to straighten, then lost himself in the smell of her. "God, you feel good. What d'you wash this in?" He nuzzled her hair. "Smells like moonbeams."

"Really drunk," she said with a sigh. "Sit down. I'll get you some coffee."

"Don't want coffee. Doesn't sober you up, only wakes you up. And I'm awake, and I have something to say to you." He drew away then, and discovered he wasn't as steady as he'd hoped. "But I'll sit down." He did, heavily. "Hate getting drunk. Haven't done it like this since I played minor league. Did I tell you I played minor league ball? Triple A."

"No." Baffled, she stood her ground and watched him.

"Right out of high school. Two years. Thought I'd make it to the show. The majors. But I didn't, so I went to college, and now I write about people who did."

"I'm sorry."

"No." He waved that away. "I like writing. Always did. Like watching the games and seeing all the little dramas. If I'd've played, I'd be nearly washed up now. I'm almost thirty-three. Old man for the game." He focused on her, smiled. "You're the most beautiful woman I've ever seen in my life. You know, the kid looks just like you. Look at him, see you. It's spooky. I see you all the time. Minding my own business, and pop! There's your face in my head. What d'ya make of that?"

"I don't know." She wanted to be angry with him, really she did. But he was so foolishly drunk. "Why don't I take you upstairs, Coop? Put you to bed."

"I want you in my bed, Zoe. I want to make love with you. I want to touch you again."

She wanted that, too. Very much. But new lines had been drawn. "You said you wanted to talk to me."

"Do you know what your skin feels like? I can't describe it, it's all soft and smooth and warm. I started thinking about your skin when I was playing poker and getting drunk tonight. I won, too. Took a big pot with a pair of sixes. Pulled in over two hundred and fifty dollars."

"Congratulations."

"But I kept thinking about you. You have this little dimple right here." He nearly poked himself in the eye, then dragged a finger down his cheek to the corner of his mouth. "I kept thinking about that little dimple, and your skin, and those big eyes and killer legs. And I kept thinking how I like to watch you with the kid, like I do sometimes from upstairs, when you don't know. Didn't know that, did you?"

"No," she said quietly. "I didn't."

"Well, see . . ." He gestured wildly.

"You've got this way of running your hand over his hair. It gets to me." He shook his head. "It really gets to me. Keenan loves me, you know. He told me he did. So did you."

"I know."

"And I meant everything I said this afternoon."

"I know." Sighing, she walked over to undo his shoelaces.

"Every word, Zoe. I've got my life set, just like I want it."

"Okay." She pried off his shoes, hefted his legs onto the couch.

"So you can stop popping into my head, 'cause it's not changing any-thing."

"I'll keep that in mind."

He was asleep before she bent over and kissed his cheek.

Chapter 10

As hangovers went, Coop knew, this would be a champ. He didn't have to open his eyes, he didn't have to move, not when his head was already beating like the army drum corps.

He wasn't sure how he'd managed to get home and into bed, but the blur of the evening wasn't comforting. Still, he thought it best to wait to tax his brain.

Cautious, close to fearful, he opened his eyes. The little face directly above him had him jerking back, then moaning at the pain.

"Good morning," Keenan said cheerfully. "Did you sleep over?"

"I don't know." Coop lifted a hand

to his head. "Where's your mother?"

"She's making my lunch. She said I could come in and look at you if I didn't wake you up. I didn't wake you up, did I? I was really quiet."

"No." Coop closed his eyes again and prayed for oblivion.

"Are you sick? Do you have a tempature?" Keenan laid a small, light hand on Coop's aching forehead. "Mama can make it better. She always makes it better." Very gently, Keenan replaced his hand with a kiss. "Does that help?"

Oh, hell, Coop thought. Even a hangover didn't have a chance against this kid. "Yeah, thanks. What time is it?"

"The big hand's on the ten and the little hand's on the eight. You can sleep in my bed until you're better, and play with my toys."

"Thanks." Coop made the supreme effort and sat up. When his head rolled, he did his best to catch it in his hands. "Keenan, be a pal and ask your mom for some aspirin."

"Okay." He raced off, and the sound of his sneakers pounding the floor had Coop shuddering.

"Headache?" Zoe asked a moment later.

Coop lifted his head. She was still in her robe. The robe he remembered from the night before. He was beginning to remember quite a bit from the night before. "If you're going to yell at me, could you do it later?"

In answer, she held out aspirin and a glass filled with reddish liquid.

"What is it?"

"A remedy from Joe the bartender.

He guarantees it'll take the edge off."

"Thanks."

There was a blast of a horn from outside that cut through Coop's skull like a dulled knife. While he was dealing with the shock of that, Keenan came racing back.

"Bye, Mama, bye!" He gave her a smacking kiss, then turned to hug Coop. "Bye."

As the door slammed behind him, Coop gulped down Joe's remedy.

"Do you want coffee?" Zoe ran her tongue around her teeth and tried not to smile. "Some breakfast?"

"You're not going to yell at me?"

"For barging in here, drunk, in the middle of the night? And for passing out on my sofa?" She paused just long enough to make her point. "No, I'm not going to yell at you. I figure you're suffering enough."

"I am, I promise you." He got up to follow her into the kitchen. "Not just physically. I feel like a total jerk."

"You *were* a total jerk." She poured a mug of coffee, set it on the table for him. "My mother's third husband had a fondness for bourbon. He swore eggs the morning after were the cure. How do you want them?"

"Scrambled would be good." He sat gingerly at the table. "I'm sorry, Zoe."

She kept her back to him. "For?"

"For being a jackass yesterday afternoon, and a bigger jackass last night."

"Oh, that." With the bacon frying, she chose a small bowl to scramble eggs in. "I don't imagine it's the first or the last time you'll be one."

"You didn't . . ." He shifted miserably. "Ah, you didn't tell Keenan I was . . ."

"Drunk and disorderly?" A half smile on her face, she glanced over her shoulder. "I told him you weren't feeling well and went to sleep on the couch. Which was close enough."

"Thanks. I wouldn't want him to think . . . you know. I don't make a habit out of it."

"So you said last night." She turned the bacon, whipped the eggs.

He watched her, gradually getting past the astonishment that she wasn't going to rub his nose in the mess he'd made of things. Remembering the afternoon before, when she'd stood up to him with all that pride and fury shining in her eyes. And the other night, when he'd fallen asleep on her couch — the way she'd looked when she slipped the boy from his arms into hers and carried him into bed.

A dozen other pictures, captured in so short a time, flitted through his head, until they were whittled down to one. This one. Zoe standing at the stove, with the morning sun streaming over her tousled hair, her robe flowing down, breakfast smells warming the room.

How could he have thought he didn't want this? Just this. And what did he do now that he knew the truth?

"Food should help." She set the plate in front of him. "I've got to get ready for work."

"Can you — Have you got a minute?"

"I suppose." She poured herself another cup of coffee. "I don't have to be in until ten."

He began to eat while thoughts scrambled in his brain. "This is good. Thanks."

"You're welcome." She leaned back against the counter. "Did you want something else?"

"Yeah." He ate more, hoping eggs equaled courage. Then he put his fork down. It was the ninth inning, he thought, and there were already two outs. "You. I want you."

She smiled a little. "Coop, I doubt you're in any shape for that, and I really have to go to work, so —"

"No, I don't mean that. I mean I do, but not —" He broke off, took a long, deep breath. "I want you to marry me."

"I beg your pardon?"

"I think you should marry me. It's a good idea." Somewhere in the back of his mind, he realized, he'd been working on this all along. He had it figured. "You can quit your night job and go back to school if you want. Or open that flower shop. Whatever. I think that's what we should do."

"Really." Because her hand was unsteady, she set her coffee down. "Well that's very generous of you, Coop, but I don't have to get married to do any of those things. So thanks just the same."

He stared. "No? You're saying no? But you love me. You said it. Twice you said it."

"We can make it three," she said evenly. "Yes, I love you. No, I won't marry you. Now I really have to get ready for work."

"Just a damn minute." Hangover forgotten, he pushed back from the table and rose. "What kind of game is this? You love me, your kid's crazy about me, we're terrific in bed, I even know how to drive a damn car pool, but you won't marry me."

"You're such an idiot. You're such a fool. Do you think because I didn't put up a struggle before I fell into your bed that you can have everything your own way? When you want it, how you want it? Well, you're wrong. And you *are* a jackass."

He winced as she stormed from the room. Strike one, he thought. And he hadn't even seen the pitch.

But the game wasn't over, he thought grimly, until the fat lady sang.

Zoe was still steaming when she

came home from work. Of all the arrogant, interfering, self-absorbed idiots she'd ever known, J. Cooper McKinnon took the gold medal. Imagine him telling her that marrying him was a good idea, then ticking off all the advantages she'd gain.

Oh, he thought he was a prize.

One day he's telling her to get any ideas of sneaking him into a relationship out of her head. As if she'd been baiting traps for him. The next he's taking pity on her and offering her a big male helping hand.

She should have bitten it off.

Not once, not once had he said what she would bring to him, what he felt for her, what he wanted. Not once had he brought up the fact that he could or would accept another man's child as his own.

She jerked open the front door, slammed it. He could take his half-baked proposal and sit on it.

"Mama! Hey, Mama!" Keenan zipped into the living room and grabbed her hand. "Come on, come on. We've got a surprise."

"What surprise? What are you doing home, Keenan? You're supposed to be at the Finklemans'."

"Coop's here." He tugged manfully on her hand. "We have a surprise. And we have a secret. And you have to come *now!*"

"All right, I'm coming." She braced herself and let Keenan drag her into the kitchen.

There were flowers, banks of them, vases and baskets overflowing on the counters, on the floor, on the windowsills. There was music, some soft, dreamy classical sonata, on the radio. The table was set, crystal she'd never seen before glinting in the sunlight, a bottle of champagne chilling in a silver bucket. And Coop was standing there, in a neatly pressed shirt and slacks.

"It's a surprise," Keenan announced gleefully. "We made everything look nice so you'd like it. And Mrs. Finkleman said we could use the glasses and the plates. And Mr. Finkleman made his special chicken 'cause it's resistible."

"Irresistible," Coop said, his eyes on Zoe. "You, ah, said you didn't need flowers and candlelight, but I've never taken you out on a date. I thought this was the next-best thing."

"Do you like it, Mama? Do you?"

"Yes, it's very nice." She bent

down to kiss Keenan. "Thank you."

"I get to go to the Finklemans' so you can have romance."

"Ah, come on, kid." Coop scooped Keenan up. "Let's get you started. You were supposed to keep quiet about it," he muttered when he carried the boy outside.

"What's romance?"

"I'll tell you later."

Satisfied with that, Keenan draped his arm around Coop's neck. "Are you gonna tell Mama the secret about us all getting married?"

"That's the plan."

"And you'll live with us and you can be my Daddy and that'll be okay?"

"That'll be great. It'll be perfect." He stopped by the fence to press a kiss to Keenan's mouth. "I love you, Keenan."

"Okay." He squeezed his arms hard around Coop's neck. "Bye."

"Bye."

"Yoo-hoo!" Mrs. Finkleman stood at the back door. She sent Coop a wink and an exaggerated thumbs-up sign before whisking Keenan inside.

She was standing pretty much where Coop had left her when he came back. He wasn't sure whether or not that was a good sign.

"So, ready for some champagne?"

"Coop, this is very nice of you, but —"

"Like the flowers?" Nervous as a cat, he popped the cork.

"Yes, they're wonderful, but —"

"I couldn't get them where you work, or I'd have spoiled the surprise. Keenan really gave me a hand setting things up." He handed her the glass, and when she was distracted, he leaned in for a slow, warm kiss. "Hi."

"Coop." She had to wait for her heart to finish its lazy somersault. "I know you must have gone to a lot of trouble —"

"I should have gone to it before. I didn't know I wanted to."

"Oh, Lord." She turned away and struggled to get her emotions under control. "I've given you the wrong impression this time. I don't need the trappings. I don't have to have romantic evenings and —" she waved toward the tapers on the table, waiting to be lit "— candlelight."

"Sure you do. So do I, when they're with you."

"You're trying to charm me," she said unsteadily. "That's new."

"You know what I am. The way this

house is set up, we've practically been living together for the past month or so. People get to know each other quicker that way than just by socializing. So you know what I am, and you fell for me anyway."

She took a drink. "You're awfully smug about it. I told you my feelings are my responsibility, and that holds true. A romantic dinner doesn't change it."

It looked like strike two, but Coop knew that if he was going to go down, he'd go down swinging. "So I want to give you a nice evening. Is something wrong with that? I want to do better than propose over scrambled eggs when I've got a hangover." His voice had risen, and he bit down on it. "Damn it, this is my first time, have a little tolerance. No, don't say anything, let me finish this. You don't need me." He took another long breath. "Not for taking care of things, for you or the kid, I mean, for mowing the grass or putting stupid barbecue grills together. What about what I need, Zoe?"

She blinked at him. "Well, that's just it. Don't you see? You made it clear that you don't need or want ties. I come with ties, Coop."

"I made it clear," he muttered. "I didn't make anything clear, because I didn't know. Didn't want to know. I was scared. There. You feel better knowing that?" He glared at her. "I was scared, because I need you. Because I need to see your face and hear your voice and smell your hair. I just need you to be there. And I need to help you mow the grass and put the grill together. I need you to need me back."

"Oh." She shut her eyes. "I like hearing that."

"Then tell me you will." He took her arms until she opened her eyes again. "It's my last swing, Zoe. Marry me."

"I —" Yes. She wanted to say yes. "It's not just me, Coop."

"You think I don't want the kid? God, open your eyes. I'm crazy about him. I fell for him before I fell for you. I want to marry both of you, then maybe have another kid or two so I can start out on the ground floor. We already worked that out."

"You — Who did what?"

He swore, stepped back, shrugged. "I kind of ran it by the kid. I figured I should smooth the way a little, and find out where he stood." When she just stared, he jammed his hands in his pockets. "It didn't seem fair not to bring him into it, since he'd be mine."

"Yours," she murmured, staring blindly into her wine.

"Since you two are a team, it would be sort of like an expansion. Anyway, he's for it. So it's two against one."

"I see."

"Maybe I don't know a lot about the daddy stuff, but I love him. That's a good start."

She looked at him again, looked into his eyes. Her heart opened, flooded. "It's a good one, all right."

"I love you." His hands relaxed in his pockets. "That's the first time I've said that to any woman — except my mother. I love you, Zoe. So why don't you marry me and give me and the kid a break?"

"It looks like I'm outvoted." She lifted a hand to his cheek.

"Is that a yes?"

"That's definitely a yes." She laughed as he swung her into his arms. "Daddy."

"I like the sound of that." He crushed his lips down on hers. "I like it a lot."

About the Author

#1 *New York Times* bestselling author **Nora Roberts** is "a word artist, painting her story and characters with vitality and verve," according to the *Los Angeles Daily News*. She has published over 140 novels, and her work has been optioned and made into films, excerpted in *Good Housekeeping* and has been translated into over twenty-five different languages and published all over the world.

In addition to her amazing success in mainstream, Nora has a large and loyal series romance audience, which took her to their hearts in 1981 with her very first book, a Silhouette Romance novel.

With over 250 million copies of her books in print worldwide and a total of 101 *New York Times* bestsellers as of 2003, twenty-nine of them reaching #1, Nora Roberts is truly a publishing phenomenon.

We hope you have enjoyed this Large Print book. Other Thorndike, Wheeler or Chivers Press Large Print books are available at your library or directly from the publishers.

For more information about current and upcoming titles, please call or write, without obligation, to:

Publisher
Thorndike Press
295 Kennedy Memorial Drive
Waterville, ME   04901
Tel. (800) 223-1244

Or visit our Web site at:
www.gale.com/thorndike
www.gale.com/wheeler

OR

Chivers Large Print
published by BBC Audiobooks Ltd
St James House, The Square
Lower Bristol Road
Bath BA2 3SB
England
Tel. +44(0) 800 136919
email: bbcaudiobooks@bbc.co.uk
www.bbcaudiobooks.co.uk

All our Large Print titles are designed for easy reading, and all our books are made to last.